Christ

The Consummation

of

Peace Forever

BY

GRACE DOLA BALOGUN

Christ the Consummation of Peace Forever
By Grace Dola Balogun

Copyright ©2014 Grace Dola Balogun

Contact Author at:
www.Gracereligiousbookspublishers.com
1-646-559-2533

Grace Religious Books Publishing & Distributors books may be ordered through booksellers or by contacting the publisher:

Grace Religious Books Publishing & Distributors, Inc.
New York
213 Bennett Avenue
New York, NY 10040

Because of the dynamic nature of the Internet, any web addresses or links contained in this book may have changed since publication and may no longer be valid. The views expressed in this work are solely those of the author and do not necessarily reflect the views of the publisher, and the publisher hereby disclaims any responsibility for them.

The author of this book does not dispense medical advice or prescribe the use of any technique as for treatment for physical, emotional, or medical problems without the advice of a physician, either directly or indirectly. The intent of the author is only to offer information of a general nature to help you in your quest for emotional and spiritual well-being. In the event you use any of the information in this book for yourself, which is your constitutional right, the author and the publisher assume no responsibility for your actions.

Soft Cover ISBN: 978-1-939415-69-1
Hard Cover ISBN: 978-1-939415-70-1

Library of Congress Control Number: 2014915229

Editing and Interior Design by CBM Christian Book Marketing www.christian-book-marketing.com

Cover Design by Lisa Hainline: www.lisahainline.com

Printed in the United States of America
Grace Religious Books Publishing & Distributors, Inc.
New York

"For to us a child is born, to us a son is given, and the government will be on His shoulders. And He will be called Wonderful Counselor, Mighty God. Everlasting Father, Prince of Peace. Of the increase of His government and peace there will be no end. He will reign on David's throne and over His kingdom, establishing and upholding it with justice and righteousness from that time on and forever. The zeal of the Lord Almighty will accomplish this" (Isaiah 9:6-7). Prophet Isaiah foretells the birth of the Messiah – Jesus Christ; the Government will be upon His shoulders and the consummation of His peace will have no end.

DEDICATION

I dedicate this book to the One and only, our Lord and Savior, Jesus Christ, who is the only consummation of peace in Heaven and in this Earth. Jesus Christ is the Prince of Peace, the Wonderful Counselor, the Almighty God, who is the only One that can bring perfect peace to this Earth upon His return.

This book is written to energize the hearts, minds, spirits and souls of all Christian denominations – even those such as: ministers, pastors, and members of all the churches' ministerial staffs to know why they are doing what they are doing because God the Father has consummated them with salvation, conformed them to the image of His Son, so that they can take the Gospel to the end of the world.

This book will educate all the people on this Earth about the plan of God and the purpose of God in the redemptive work which is from the beginning of the consummation of peace of the entire world. The book will help all the believing Christians to know the peace of consummation and the righteousness of God through His Son, Jesus Christ.

In reading this book, people will learn that Christ alone is the source of peace on this Earth. Jesus Christ is the consummation of the New Covenant of peace, which was sealed with His presence before the foundation of this world. Believers will know how to maintain perfect peace by learning how to maintain a right relationship with the Lord.

This book is an eye-opener to all the believing Christians who will read it. They will find out that God the Father has established a covenant of peace through Jesus Christ from the Old Testament to the New Testament. God's peace came to the world through Jesus Christ's death and resurrection. This book is therefore recommended for mature and new believers alike.

"Jesus Christ was praying in a certain place. One day when He was finished, one of His disciples said to Him, 'Lord, teach us to pray.' 'He said to them, 'When you pray, say, Father hallowed be your name, your kingdom come. Give us each day our daily bread. Forgive us our sins, for we also forgive everyone who sins against us. And lead us not into temptation' "(Luke 11:1-4). Believing Christians must learn how to pray for all life's necessary provisions based on Christian principles. We must pray such petitions according to God's will and according to His glory.

Preface

Christ is the consummation of peace; He came to this world in our own form (in the flesh just like every human being). He redeemed humanity from their past, present and future sins. God the Father Almighty gave people of this world the forgiveness of sin through the atonement of Jesus Christ's sacrifice. He is the Lamb of God who took away the sin of the whole world. Christ Jesus bought all the people in this world with the consummation of peace by His resurrection and the gift of eternal life.

God the Father, by His grace, after we gave our life to Christ offers grace and salvation. We become the adopted children of God and receive the inheritance as a child of God. Jesus Christ is our Mediator of a New Covenant and through Jesus Christ we are able to approach the throne of grace bodily and pray to the Father through Jesus Christ, His Son. Christ Jesus is our Great Intercessor in Heaven as He is seated at the right hand of God the Father praying for those who believe in Him a prayer that can never be uttered.

Jesus Christ is our consummation of peace; He is coming back to judge the quick and the dead and all eyes shall see Him. Jesus Christ is our hope of glory, believe in Him and you will have eternal life and live with Him in Heaven forever. Jesus Christ is also our consummation of peace in regards to our living faith in Him. He blessed believers by baptizing them and all those who will believe in Him with the indwelling power of the Holy Spirit. Jesus Christ wants everyone on this Earth to be saved and come to the knowledge of repentance and pray for forgiveness, which is only in Him. Jesus Christ is our consummation of peace; He gave believers the victory over sin and death, and over Satan. Believers are no longer slaves of sin; they are slaves of righteousness. God the Father imputed Christ's righteousness to all those who are living lives of obedience to the Father's commandments and daily living in the Word of God.

Jesus Christ is the believers' consummation of peace because He cares for the lowly, the lonely, and the afflicted, distressed, those who are sick and those who are in trouble with many diverse diseases. Christ cares for them; He prays for them, interceding for them at the right hand of God. Jesus Christ is our consummation of peace because He is the way, the truth and the life. Christ is the true light that shines in the darkness and the darkness comprehended it not. Christ is the Father's glory, and the Son forevermore. He will bring peace to a new Heaven and a new earth where righteousness will dwell and abide forever. When He returns to establish His Kingdom, His consummation of peace will be fully complete. He will then return everything to God the Father, and God the Father will be all in all.

Christ is our consummation of peace because in Him there is true happiness; through the power of the Holy Spirit, He helps us to know true happiness. He teaches us to abide in Him and He Himself will abide in us. Christ is the consummation of peace, who guides His sheep. He is a good Shepherd; He will never fail nor forsake His sheep. Christ is the Good Shepherd; He will put the weak and distressed sheep on His shoulders and bring them to the pasture where all the sheep will be one in Him and where He is the one Shepherd, in the one universe.

"Then Jesus told them this parable, ' Suppose one of you has a hundred sheep and loses one of them. Does He not leave the ninety-nine in the open country and go after the lost sheep until He finds it? And when He finds it, He joyfully puts it on His shoulders and goes home. Then He calls His friends and neighbors together and says: Rejoice with me; I have found my lost sheep. I tell you that in the same way there will be more rejoicing in Heaven over one sinner who repents than over ninety-nine righteous persons who do not need to repent" (Luke 15:3-7). Jesus Christ was telling us that God and the angels in Heaven have such love, compassion and grief for those who have fallen into sin and spiritual death that when one sinner repents, they openly rejoice in God's love for sinners.

CONTENTS

"Yet, O Lord, you are our Father. We are the clay, you are the potter; we are all the work of your hand. Do not be angry beyond measure, O Lord; do not remember our sins forever. Oh, look upon us, we pray, for we are all your people" (Isaiah 64:8-9). God the Father Almighty responded to Prophet Isaiah's prayer by describing His continual appeal to the rebellious nation to return to Him. God is calling people of this Earth today through Jesus Christ, His Son.

Chapter One

Christ the Consummation of Peace in the Old Testament

Consummation means the completing, or the perfection as well as the fulfillment of promise; the consummation of one's life works. Jesus Christ, the consummation of peace means the perfection or the completion of peace. Jesus Christ is our consummation of peace from the Old Testament Scripture. Prophet Isaiah prophesies 800 years before Christ: "For to us a child is born, to us a son is given, and the government will be on His shoulders. And He will be called Wonderful Counselor, Mighty God Everlasting Father, and Prince of Peace. Of the increase of His government and peace there will be no end. He will reign on David's throne and over His kingdom, establishing and upholding it with justice and righteousness from that time on and forever. The zeal of the Lord Almighty will accomplish this" (Isaiah 9:6-7).

Isaiah prophesied the birth of Jesus Christ the Messiah and that His birth will come at a definite time and place in history of this world, to include that this Messiah would be born in a unique way. Isaiah gave the people the four names that will characterize, or proved His function as the Messiah. Christ will exercise His consummation of peace as a Wonderful Counselor; the Messiah will perform and show His supernatural wonder, and perform miracles.

The Messiah will show His character by His work healing and His teaching of the Word of God. As a Wonderful Counselor, He will be the Son incarnation of perfect wisdom, peace with the words of eternal life; as a counselor He would disclose the perfect plan of salvation. The Scripture confirmed: "Therefore, the Lord Himself will give you a sign: The virgin will be with child and will give birth to a son, and will call Him Emmanuel" (Isaiah 7:14). The sign that was given to Isaiah was "Virgin" which means a new bride, who would have been a virgin until the time of her marriage. The prophecy's ultimate fulfillment was come to pass in the birth of Jesus Christ by the Virgin Mary. Mary was a virgin, and she remained a virgin after the birth of Jesus Christ. Mary's conception of her Son came by a miracle of the Holy Spirit. The child was called Emmanuel that means "God with us," which also means God's one and only Son. In the Messiah all the fullness of the Deity exists in a bodily form.

Christ is the consummation of peace as the everlasting Father. He not only came to reveal our heavenly Father to us, but He Himself will act toward His people eternally as a compassionate Father who loves, protects and supplies all the needs of His children. Christ as the consummation of peace is the Prince of Peace. His rule will bring peace with God for human beings through the deliverance from sin and death. Jesus Christ's reign on Earth will establish with no distinction and it was made between His first and Second Coming. Christ's redemptive work and rule is seen as occurring in one distant coming. Prophet Isaiah's prophecy revealed that Jesus Christ's rule on Earth will involve the first and second and will reach advent in history of the world. Isaiah's prophecy will reach its consummation at the Second Coming of Jesus Christ.

The Messiah is called Wonderful Counselor, which means the Messiah is incomprehensible. Jesus is wonderful in a way that made people's mind shake when they see His work and miracles. A counselor a wise ruler or King that gives guidance to His people and is excellent in wisdom. Christ is a wise counselor of consummation of peace. We see in the Old Testament according to the

Scripture: "Men of all nations came to listen to Solomon's wisdom, sent by all the kings of the world, who had heard of His wisdom." King Solomon was given a tremendous godly wisdom that eventually turned from the Lord to serve other gods. We can see clearly that to have wisdom and to follow wisdom is two different issues. Solomon's greatest failure was that He did not apply His own spiritual wisdom to every area of His life. Even though, He was the wisest man on Earth during His time, He did not live as wisely as some of God's faithful people.

The Scripture says that: "He will judge between many peoples and will settle disputes for strong nations far and wide. They will beat their swords into plowshares and their spears into pruning hooks. Nation will not take up sword against nation, nor will they train for war anymore. Every man will sit under His own vine and under His own fig tree and no one will make them afraid, for the Lord Almighty has spoken. All the nations may walk in the name of their gods; we will walk in the name of the Lord our God for ever and ever" (Micah 4:3-5). Prophet Micah also prophesies the time when Christ in God or God in Christ will rule over the entire universe. It will be a time of happiness, goodness and peace. God Almighty will be honored and worshiped not only in Israel, but in all the nations of the Earth. This prophesies of the future kingdom of God will begin when Jesus Christ returns in His Second Coming to destroy all evil and to establish His righteous reign on Earth.

People of this Earth must live for God the three in one. While waiting for God's Kingdom to come to the Earth in all its fullness. We must walk in His righteous ways and witness to the people in all the nations to let them know Christ's consummation of peace. This is a mystery which God through prophet Micah shows that the people of God shall incorporate a new way of spiritual worship which shall be established with better privileges that shall be granted. In this way a better provision will be made for the establishing the Kingdom of God among the people of the world. Church shall be set up in all the nations of Earth, whereby the Lord Jesus Christ the consummation of peace, will peacefully be adding daily those people who shall be saved. Jesus Christ Himself as the consummation of peace will build the Church upon a rock that shall never be shaken or moved.

Prophet Isaiah was one the great prophet in the Old Testament. He was called by God and anointed with the power of the Holy Spirit. The Scripture revealed: "I heard the voice of the Lord saying, whom I shall send?

And who will go for us? And I said, 'Here am I, send me!' He said, 'Go and tell this people be ever hearing but never understanding, be ever seeing, but never perceiving" (Isaiah 6:8-9). Prophet Isaiah was commissioned as a prophet after he cleansed His mouth and His heart; he was made fit to stay remaining in the presence of the Lord and his sins were forgiven and his heart was cleansed by the Holy Spirit.   Isaiah responded to the call of God immediately, just as Jesus Christ gave the Apostles the Great Commission to proclaim the Gospel of salvation of God to the whole world.

God told Isaiah that the people of Israel will reject His message; His preaching might even turn them more against God. Nevertheless, Isaiah must remain faithful and preach faithfully about the unwelcome message of the judgment of the Lord. God the Father encouraged Prophet Isaiah that a small remnant of the people of Israel will believe and be preserved and be saved. God revealed to the Prophet Isaiah His plan of salvation for the world, the New Covenant, where God will judge an apostate church and where or at the same time, rise up holy people that will remain faithful to Him and His Word. Prophet Isaiah's message emphasized the nature of God, the power of God and the holiness of God. He declared that God is the

Creator, the Almighty Ruler of this Earth. Everything that happens in the world is according to God's ultimate purposes of salvation and judgment, and the repentance of sins. God is holy, righteous and just; His holiness is ordained and tempered by His mercy, He is full of patience and slow to anger.

God is holy by nature; He requires His children to be separated as the holy one of the Lord, and moreover, God wants His children to be obedient to His commandments. Prophet Isaiah revealed His message of hope concerning the coming of the Messiah. He knew that God would fulfill the Abraham Covenant and His promises through all the faithful remnant of the people of Israel. The Messiah will come, and through Him, God Almighty will offer the salvation to all the people in this world. During Prophet Isaiah's time on Earth he was looking forward to the future of Messianic age. The Prophet Isaiah therefore prophesied that Christ is a consummation of peace for all.

"Behold, I will create new Heaven and a new Earth. The former things will not be remembered, nor will they come to mind. But be glad and rejoice forever in what I will create, for I will create Jerusalem to be a delight and its people a joy. I will rejoice over Jerusalem and take delight in my people; the sound of weeping and of crying will be heard in it no more" (Isaiah 65:17-19). Isaiah's prophecy foresees God's future kingdom on Earth. Isaiah blends the age of eternity where sin and death will be no more with the Messianic age, the millennial kingdom; there will indeed be a new Heaven and a new Earth. God has plans for the present Jerusalem in His millennial kingdom.

Chapter Two

Christ the Consummation of Peace
in the New Testament

The Scripture revealed: "Therefore, the Lord Himself will give you a sign: The virgin will be with child and will give birth to a son, and will call Him Emmanuel" (Isaiah 7:14). The prophet prophesies that in God's name, giving them a sign in general of His good will to the people of Israel and to the House of David, to the nations to your family, the Messiah is to be born, and you will not be able to destroy His blessing if it is truly in you. Born of a virgin who signifies both the divine power and the divine purity with which He shall be brought into the universe. The Messiah shall be introduced in a glorious way; He will be wrapped up in His glorious name which shall be Emmanuel - God with us, God comes in our own nature, God is at peace with His creation, and is in a covenant with His people. If the Messiah had not been Emmanuel - God with us, He could not have been Jesus Christ - the Savior of the world.

Jesus Christ the One and only, the consummation of peace - He is the strongest consolation in the time of trouble, our relationship to Him, our interest in Him, and our expectations of Him and from Him. The Messiah is the great light that visits those that sat in the darkness and He is the one that bring deliverance to the captives and the oppressed. The design of the Gospel of God is to break the yoke of the bondage of sin and Satan, to remove the burden of the guilt and corruption that we might have been brought into because of the glorious liberty as the children of God. Prophet Isaiah revealed to us that Messiah Emmanuel will accomplish great things for us. The child is born because the church before His incarnation received great benefit and great advantage - He was the Lamb of God that was slain, in the same way He was a child born from the foundation of the world.

All the great things that God the Father did for the Old Testament church were done by Christ as the eternal Word of God, and for His sake as the mediator of a New Covenant, especially for the people of Israel. The same Christ who is the Mighty God became a child born of Virgin Mary. He humbled Himself and emptied Himself in order to exalt Himself to bless the believers. The Word became flesh and dwelt in our world. Christ is born to us, Christ is given to us as the Son of God, and the Son of man. He was invested with the highest honor and power so that we know Him and honor Him as Christ, our friend. Jesus Christ is wonderful because He was both God and man. He was called "Counselor" because He was intimately acquainted with the counsels of God from eternity, and He gives counsel to the children of God. He is Jesus, which is the wisdom of the Father, and is made of God to us wisdom. Christ has wisdom as well as strength; He was able to save to the uttermost those who believe in Him.

Jesus Christ is the everlasting Father, the Father of Eternity; He is God, one with the Father, who is from everlasting to everlasting. Christ is the author and finisher of our faith; He is also the author of the everlasting life and happiness to those that the Father blessed; He is the Prince of peace, and He preserves, commands, and creates peace in His Kingdom. His throne is above every throne and His kingdom is peace that will have no end. Christ the consummation of peace will bear the burden of the government of all the nations of this world. Jesus Christ's church shall be multiplied, shall increase, and shall shine more and more brightly in this entire world. Therefore,

Christ's consummation of peace system shall be a peaceable government that will be more agreeable according to His riches in glory as the Prince of Peace. Christ shall rule His Kingdom with love, and His government will increase as the peace shall also increase.

"Never again will there be in it an infant who lives but a few days, or an old man who does not live out His years; He who dies at a hundred will be though a mere youth; He who fails to reach a hundred will be considered accursed" *(Isaiah 65:20).* *Although death will exist in the Messianic kingdom.* *Life spans will be much longer than they are now.* *A hundred year old will still be considered a youth and those who die before that age will be considered accursed.*

Chapter 3

Christ the Consummation of Peace:
The Word of God Became Flesh

Jesus Christ became the consummation of peace when He came to the world in our human form. The Scripture revealed: "In the beginning was the Word, and the Word was with God, and the Word was God. He was with God in the beginning. Through Him all things were made; without Him nothing was made that has been made. In Him was life, and that life was the light of men. The light shines in the darkness, but the darkness has not understood it" (John 1:1-5). In the Gospel of John - John called Jesus Christ, "The Word of God," and as such, John presented Christ Jesus as the personal Word of God that indicated that in these last days God has been spoken to the people in the word of peace through the one and only Son of God, and the consummation of peace to the people of this world.

Jesus Christ is the manifold wisdom of God. "It is because of Him that you are in Christ Jesus, who has become for us wisdom from God that is, our righteousness. Therefore, as it is written: Let Him who boasts, boast in the Lord" (1st Corinthians 1:30-31). Jesus Christ came because of us and all the people in the world that have not been converted or received salvation; therefore, Christ became the wisdom from God. It is through Jesus Christ, in Christ and with Christ that all those who believe in Jesus Christ receives wisdom from God the Father as well as experiences righteousness, sanctification and redemption.

Immediately after a person is joined with Jesus Christ, and surrendered their life to Him, Christ becomes the source of all their blessings. And they become the perfect revelation of the nature and person of God. Just as a person's words reveals His or her heart and mind, Christ as the Word reveals the heart and mind of God the Father to His children. Jesus Christ was the Word of God in relation to the Father. Christ was pre-existent with God the Father before the creation of the universe. He was a person existing from eternity, distinct from, but in eternal fellowship with God the Father. Christ was divine - the Word was God, having the same nature and essence as the Father. Christ as the Word of God in relation to the world.

It was through Jesus Christ that God the Father created the universe as well as sustains the universe. Jesus Christ became the Word of God in relation to His humanity. The Word became flesh - the Son of God put on human nature, but without sin.

This is the true statement of revelation of the incarnation: Jesus Christ came down from Heaven and entered the way of human condition of life through the form of human birth and became fully God and fully man. Jesus Christ was not created; Christ is eternal, conceived by the power of the Holy Spirit and born of the Virgin Mary. Jesus Christ has always been in loving fellowship with God the Father and the Holy Spirit. Jesus Christ was the true light of the life of people on Earth. He is the true, genuine life, which is embodied in Christ. Jesus Christ is the life and light for everyone in the world. God the Father's truth, God's nature, and God's power were made available to all the people in the world through Him.

Jesus Christ is the consummation of peace who produced the light that shines in an evil and sinful world, which was controlled by Satan. Many people in the world have not received the salvation of God which is in Christ alone by faith, nor have they accepted Christ's life, nor His light, but the darkness has covered them, also the darkness has not completely won them over. Jesus Christ illumines all who hear His Gospel by imparting a measure of grace and understanding in order that they may freely chose to accept or reject the message of the Gospel. Apart from Jesus Christ's light, there is no other light by which people of this Earth may see the truth of the Gospel and be saved into His Holy hands.

"And I, because of their actions and their imaginations, I am about to come and gather all nations and tongues, and they will come and see my glory. I will set a sign among them, and I will send some of those who survive to the nations – to Tarshish, to the Libyans and Lydians (famous as archers), to Tubal and Greece, and to the distant islands that have not heard of my fame or seen my glory. They will proclaim my glory among the nations" (Isaiah 66:18-19). *Believers from all nations will be gathered to see the glory of God. After they have survived His judgment, they will be sent to the nations to bring all the remaining Jews to the Lord, the God of Israel, the gathering will occur at the end of the age.*

Chapter 4

Christ the Consummation of Peace was Born in a Manger

Jesus Christ is the consummation of Peace. He is the "Baby in a Manger" from the time that Angel Gabriel announces His conception. The Scripture revealed: "In the sixth month God sent Angel Gabriel to Nazareth, a town in Galilee, to a virgin pledged to be married to a man named Joseph, a descendant of David. The virgin's name was Mary, the angel went to her and said, 'Greetings, you who are highly favored! The Lord is with you. You will be with child and give birth to a son, and you are to give Him the name Jesus. He will be great and will be called the Son of the most high. The Lord God will give Him the throne of His father David, and He will reign over the house of Jacob forever; His kingdom will never end' " (Luke 1:26-28, 31-33). Jesus Christ has been the consummation of peace since the angel announces His conception to Virgin Mary.

While Mary was highly favored above all the women on Earth during that time, she was chosen by God to be the mother of Jesus Christ. Mary was chosen because He found favor with God; her humbleness and her godly life pleased God to the point that God chose her for this most important task.

Mary's blessings brought her great joy until today. Jesus Christ was conceived by the power of the Holy Spirit and Christ came to the world with peace because He is the Prince of Peace. Therefore, Jesus Christ was holy and He was called the Holy Child of Bethlehem. Christ the consummation of peace to the world brought joy to all the people in the world. Jesus Christ is the wisdom of God, and the power of God. Mary was full of joy and she sang a song to God: "And Mary said: My soul glorified the Lord and my spirit rejoices in God my savior. For He has been mindful of the humble state of His servant. From now on all generations will call me blessed for the mighty one has done a great things for me, holy is His name" (Luke 1:46-49). Mary rejoiced and was glad that the Lord was going to use her to bring His Son to the world.

Mary submitted herself completely to God's will for her life as well as she believed in Angel Gabriel's message. Mary willingly accepted the honor and the reproach that will come to her being the mother of the Holy Child. Believers who are young men and women should follow Mary and Joseph's example by living a life of purity before marriage; love for God, faith in His Word, with a willingness to be obedient to the command of the Holy Spirit. Virgin Mary after the angel left her recognizes her own need of salvation. She was a sinner who needed Jesus Christ as her Savior. The idea that Mary herself was immediately conceived and lived a sinless life is nowhere taught in the Scripture. Angel Gabriel said to Mary, "You highly favored of God," which means God has desires, in His choice to make Mary the mother of the Messiah; God made her a partaker in the redemptive work of the Earth. Mary has the blessing of God upon her since she was born, because she separated herself to serve the Lord, to be at the presence of the Lord at all time. Even though Mary was poor not rich, but yet God chose her to have the honor to be the mother of the Messiah, the Savior of the people on Earth.

This is the reason why that when Christ was born, the angel announced His birth and says: "And there were shepherds living out in the fields nearby, keeping watch over their flocks at night, an angel of the Lord appeared to them, and the glory of the Lord shone around them, and they were terrified. But the Angel said to the shepherds, 'Do not be afraid, I bring you good news of great joy that will be for all the people. Today in the town of David a Savior has been born to you; He is Christ the Lord. This will be a sign to you: You will find a baby wrapped in clothes and lying in a manger.' Suddenly a great company of the heavenly host appeared with the angels, praising God and saying, glory to God in the highest, and on Earth peace to men on whom His favor rests" (Luke 2:8-14). Jesus Christ came to the world as a consummation of peace. The angel and all the heavenly host were rejoicing and proclaimed peace on Earth through the birth of Jesus Christ. Jesus Christ was born in a stable, a place where animals were kept. The stable could even be called a cave, or manger, a feeding place for animals.

The birth of Jesus Christ, the Savior, is the greatest event in all the history of the universe, which occurred in a most humble way. Jesus was a baby in the manger; He was the King of kings, the Lord of lords, and the God of gods. He was neither born nor did He live like a king in this universe. God's people are kings and priests, but in this life we must be like Christ - humble ourselves and live a simple life. Jesus as the consummation of peace was called by the angels a Savior, as a Savior, Christ has come to bless

His people with His peace. He has come to deliver us from our sins, and from the domains of darkness of Satan into His marvelous light, and as well as deliver us from ungodly people in the world, from world of fear, death and from the condemnation of our transgressions.

Christ our Savior is also Christ our Lord. He has been anointed as the Messiah of God and the Lord who rules over His people. No one can give their life to Jesus as their Savior without submitting to the Lordship of Jesus Christ. When Christ Jesus was born in a manger no one could believe that He was the Messiah, the true Son of God. But there attended His birth with angels and all the heavenly host choir, then it proved to us that this type of announcement cannot be done for an ordinary person in this world; it can only be done for the Son of God. Even the wise men that were Gentiles notice through the star that shone to them from Heaven. The shepherds who were abiding in the fields, keeping watch over their flocks by night were employed to witness the birth of Jesus Christ the consummation of peace.

The angels were sent to the shepherds in the field, not to King Herod and the rulers of the Synagogues, priests or elders. The shepherds were not sleeping at night, they were wide-awake, and therefore, they cannot be deceived of what they heard and what they saw. The shepherd was employed then, not in the acts of devotion, but in the business of their honest calling by God the Father to witness the birth of God the Son. The angels give glory to God whose kindness and love has designed this favor, and whose infinite wisdom has done it. All the work of God is for His glory from the beginning of creation, but the redemptive work of the world is for His glory in the highest.

Christ who is the peace on Earth when He was born is also the peace and goodwill to the people of the world. Christ is at peace with His people that He created and we have peace with God when we receive His salvation and the gift of grace through Jesus Christ. All the good we have, all the hope we have, we received it, and owed to God the Father's goodwill. Therefore, if we have the comfort of God's goodwill, God receives the glory of His goodwill. We have to know that the goodwill of God towards His people on this Earth is always to His glory in the highest, and also, always accompanies with peace to all God's people on Earth. Christ was the consummation of peace since the first day that He was born on this Earth. Glory be to God, Hosanna in the highest.

"When I consider your heavens, the work of your fingers, the moon and the stars, which you have set in place, what is man that you are mindful of Him, the son of man that you care for Him? You made Him a little lower than the heavenly beings and crowned Him with glory and honor" (Psalm 8:3-6). This psalm expresses the amazing honor that God has bestowed on humankind, it affirms that we as humans were created by God for a glorious purpose, we are not just animals, the product of natural evolution and chance. We are so valuable to God that we are special object of His concern and favor.

Chapter 5

Christ the Consummation of Peace for the Forgiveness of Sins

When Jesus Christ was on the Cross; the Scripture revealed: "Jesus said, Father, forgive them, for they do not know what they are doing. And they divided up His clothes by casting lots" (Luke 23: 34). The first saying of Jesus Christ on the Cross on the day of crucifixion and His death was the love and the foundation of God the Father's plan of redemption. Jesus who was born sinless, God divine and human, who had never sinned, died on behalf of and in the place of sinful humanity in the world. Jesus Christ's crucifixion was the penalty for humanity's sin, which was paid by Jesus Christ's precious blood in order to redeem us from the power of Satan. The gates of Heaven are open for all the people who turn to God in repentance and faith, and receive the forgiveness of sins and eternal life.

Jesus Christ prayed for His enemies; He told the Father to forgive them. Christ Jesus says seven remarkable words after He was nailed on the tree. Just before He died, this is His first word where He prayed for those who crucified Him. During the time they were fastening Him to the Cross, and when they were nailing Him to the Cross, He never stopped praying for all His adversaries, collectively Jesus wants us to be imitators of Him while on Earth He told us to pray for our enemies. Christ gave us this example while He was on the Cross and His first spoken words were prayer for those who crucified Him.

Jesus Christ today is at the right hand of God the Father. He continues to make intercession for our transgressions on all our transgressors, a prayer that can never be uttered. Jesus Christ's words on the Cross, as well as His sufferings, His death on the Cross, purchased and procured for humanity the forgiveness of sins. The blood of Jesus Christ shed on the Cross speaks for forgiveness to the Father.

Jesus Christ said that, "For they know not what they do," because if they knew that they were persecuting the Messiah, the Son of God, they would not have crucified Him. Those who crucified Jesus Christ were so ignorant, they were lacking of knowledge and proper instruction of what was written in the Old Testament Scriptures. Moreover, they believed the Synagogue Ruler who is full of prejudiced against Christ instead of reading the Word of God, find out the fact on their own. Therefore, by persecuting and crucifying Jesus Christ they thought that they were doing God a favorable service. Christ felt sorry and pitied them and prayed for them.

Believing Christians must pray and call on God the Father, Son and the Holy Spirit in begging Him for our own ignorance and the ignorance of others and pray for repentance and for forgiveness of sins. We must be able to pray for our enemies at all times; and pray for those who hate us and persecute us. We must also be earnest with God in prayer for forgiveness of our enemies' sins, which are their sins against us. If Jesus Christ prays for His enemies, who are we that we cannot follow His example and pray for our enemies who persecute us, despise and plan evils against us. If Jesus Christ loved and prayed for His enemies, there are no enemies we have that we are not obliged to love and pray for them.

We have to remember the conversion of the thief on the side of Jesus that was crucified with Him. There are two thieves, but one of them repents and is converted. These two thieves represented the different effects and how the people of this Earth will take the Gospel, which the Cross of Jesus Christ means to the people of the world. Some people will see the Cross of Jesus Christ to be a Savior of life unto life, while other people will see the Cross of Jesus Christ as death unto death. The Cross of Christ is the Cross of eternal life. Our Lord Jesus Christ said: "For if you forgive men when they sin against you, your heavenly Father will also forgive you. But if you do not forgive men their sins, your Father will not forgive your sins" (Matthew 6:14-15). Jesus Christ is the consummation of peace in forgiveness; He emphasizes that all believing Christians must be ready and willing with an open heart to forgive the offences of others.

If we are unwilling to forgive those who do us wrong, God will not forgive us our transgressions and our prayers will not avail to Him. This is a very important principle that all believers must be able to abide; it is one of the most important in part of the Christian doctrine. The Scripture says: "The true light that gives light to every man was coming into the world" (John 1:9). Jesus Christ illumines all who hear His Gospel by imparting a measure of grace and understanding of the love, which the Father bestowed upon believers through Jesus Christ His only begotten Son.

Christ in all His teaching emphasizes that we must love our neighbor, love those who hate us, love our enemies, and do good to those who persecute us. By doing this we are showing the proof of Christ like character in our lives and we are complete in Him. The teaching of Jesus Christ during His Earthly ministry continues also in the Scripture: "But I tell you: love your enemies and pray for those who persecuted you, that you may be sons of your Father in Heaven. He causes His Sun to rise on the evil and the good, and sends rain on the righteous and the unrighteous" (Matthew 5:44-45). During Jesus' earthly ministry some people wrongly believed that it was okay to hate their enemy.

Even in the Old Testament according to the Law of Moses no one must use the word "hate" for an enemy. Instead Moses called the people to be kind-hearted even towards the pets of their enemy. The Law commanded that people must love their neighbors, strangers and to those resident alien that they do not know where they come from: "If you come across your enemy's ox or donkey wandering off, be sure to take it back to Him. If you see the donkey of someone who hates you fallen down under its load, do not leave it there; be sure you help Him with it" (Exodus 23:24). Jesus Christ said that it is the duty of believers to love their enemy. Even though some people are very bad and wicked in that they plan so many things against us, yet that does not discharge us from the great debt we owed to our Lord's command, which is to love them. We must love our enemies with Christ's love, with an open mind, forgiving them of their wrongful deeds against us.

In the book of Prophet Isaiah, God spoke to His people: "Come now, let us reason together, says the Lord. Though your sins are like scarlet, they shall be as white as snow; though they are read as crimson, they shall be like wool" (Isaiah 1:18). God called His people again and again through the prophets in the Old Testament; God is calling us today through Jesus Christ His only begotten Son full of truth and grace. God does not want to condemn and destroy His people. God the Father offered forgiveness and pardon if people would only repent and pray ask for forgiveness of their sins, putting down all their evil ways, and begin to do good, as well as obey His Word. God's forgiveness is now and is always available for all who, though they have sinned, confess their sins repent and accept God's cleansing through the blood of Jesus Christ.

Those who refuse God's mercy and choose to continue with their wickedness, as well as continue in their rebellious ways, will be destroyed. God the Father through

Jesus Christ atoning blood can purge away our sins and bless us with a new life in Him. Jesus Christ is the consummation of peace to those who repent of their sins and surrender their life to His Lordship forever. The Scripture revealed, "Praise the Lord, O my Soul, and forget not all His benefits who forgives all your transgressions, sins and heals all your diseases, who redeems your life from the pit and crowns you with love and compassion" (Psalm 103:3-4). The fall of Adam and Eve brought sin into human being and the human race with the universal experience of sin, sickness and death.

One of the most important blessings of God to the human race is forgiveness of their sins, healing their diseases, and the gift of redemption and eternal life. Forgiveness of sins is the first and most important, most valuable gift we can receive from God. Through God the Son and God the Holy Spirit restored believing Christians to God and redeemed them from destruction. Healing of diseases that come to us because of sin and Satan is likewise part of the salvation that God makes available to His children and the people of the world.

After we repent and confess our sins, we ask for forgiveness of our sins; the Lord washes us clean from all our transgressions, our prayer will rise to Heaven, and He will hear our prayers and answer our prayers if He knows that what we asked for in prayer is good for us and it is according to His will for us. Therefore, repentance, confession, forgiveness of sins is very important in the life of all believing Christians. Therefore, the Lord said, "As far as the east is from the West, so far has He removed our transgressions from us. As a father has compassion on His children, so the Lord has compassion on those who fear Him" (Psalm 103:12-13). God always shows His compassion to those who forsake their wicked ways and turn to Him.

He showed mercy to all those who truly loved Him and fear Him. The fear of God, the awareness of God in our lives is a redeeming fear that motivates believers to turn away from evil and keep God's Word and commandment in their hearts. The fear of the Lord God Almighty makes believers to keep all God's precepts, and to seek the Lord's face, get closer and closer nearer and nearer to Him every day. The fear of the Lord help believers to receive the grace of God, the blessings that God gives to those who fear Him, to receive His mercy, love and forgiveness; moreover, the true fear of God helps believers to receive His fatherly love and compassion, His faithfulness and goodness as His children.

In forgiveness God has compassion because He knows our weakness and our infirmities. All those who gave their life to Jesus Christ are in need of His compassion. As a father has deep compassion for His children when they fail, suffer or when they are mistreated by someone, in the same way our heavenly Father also has compassion when His own children are hurting in the middle of worldly trouble, failures and struggles. We must not think that our heavenly Father is uncaring or He does not know what we are going through; rather we must remember that His eyes look unto us and are watching us with compassion and He will help us according to His will and according to our need. Forgiveness of God helps us to know Him better and stay in His Word and He blesses us with Christ the consummation of peace in forgiveness.

"The Lord reigns forever; He has established His throne for judgment.   He will judge the world in righteousness; I will govern the peoples with justice.   The Lord is a refuge for the oppressed, a stronghold in times of trouble.   Those who know your name will trust in you for you, Lord, have never forsaken those who seek you" (Psalm 9:7-9).   Believing Christians must give thanks and praises to the Lord because He will one day fully deliver those who seek Him and He will bring judgment against His enemies.

Chapter 6

Christ the Consummation of Peace
of the Grace of God

Jesus Christ is the consummation of peace of the grace of God. The Scripture revealed clearly, "For God was pleased to have all His fullness dwell in Him, and through Him to reconcile to Himself all things, whether things on Earth or things in Heaven, by making peace through His blood, shed on the Cross" (Colossians 1:19-20). Christ lives to make peace in Heaven and in this Earth. The Deity of Jesus Christ was plainly emphasized in all the Scripture the Word of God. The full and complete Godhead with all that it represents dwell in Jesus Christ - We see in another Scripture: "For in Christ all the fullness of the Deity lives in bodily form, and you have been given fullness in Christ, who is the head over every power and authority" (Colossians 2:9-10). Jesus Christ is the fullness of abundance life for all those who believe in Him.

All fullness dwells in Jesus Christ and it was the plan of God the Father before the creation of the universe. The work of redemption was completed and finished through Jesus Christ wherein there is the remission of our sins. We are redeemed from our sin by Christ's forgiveness by God's grace of salvation. Jesus Christ is our mediation of reconciliation who procures peace as well as a pardon for all sinners; He will bring all who are holy creatures into one blessed body at the end of the age. The greatest enemies of God, the haters of God will be reconciled, through Jesus Christ's atonement and His blood will atone for their sins when they make peace with God through repentance and salvation through Jesus Christ. Jesus Christ is the peace between God and man through His blood that was shed on the Cross. The Gospel of God through Jesus Christ is open to all the people in the world, no one should exclude themselves.

The great concern of those who have received Christ is to walk, and abide in Him. Believers must walk with Christ daily and maintain good communion with Him. The more believers' daily walk with Jesus Christ, the more they are rooted and established in their faith. Those who are in Jesus Christ, those who fully believe in Him, will dwell in Him in spirit, soul, and body. The fullness of the three Godhead will also dwell in them through Christ. They will dwell in Jesus Christ in a bodily form and they will be doing what is pleasing to Him from this Earth to Heaven. Those who are fully in Jesus Christ will be perfect, completely spiritually matured; they will maintain a good relationship with God the Father who loved them fully through Jesus Christ.

Believing Christians will be glad to seek God's will and do His will; they will love the Lord and love other people around them. The Scripture says, "But about the Son He says, your throne, O God, will last forever and ever, and righteousness will be the scepter of your kingdom" (Hebrews 1:8). God was referring to Jesus, that He is higher than the angels; Christ is the Son and eternal King in Heaven. He is higher than all the angels of God because Jesus Christ is the Son of God. Jesus Christ came to this world righteously to the scepter and throne; He was in perfection of His righteousness.

Christ came to put to an end transgressions, and to make an end of sin, which is the most hateful and as well as hurtful things in the world. God's expression of the office of Jesus Christ and how Christ was qualified for the office of mediator are confirmed. Jesus Christ is the anointed Messiah. He was anointed with the oil of gladness, the joy which was set forth before Him as the reward of His service and sufferings, that crown of glory and gladness, which He will wear forever after the suffering of death.

The anointing of Jesus Christ was above the anointing of the angles in Heaven. It pleases the Father to pour out the spirit of anointing upon Him without measure. Jesus Christ, who is the omnipotence, was declared as the creator of the world and the changer of the world. "From the fullness of His grace we have all received one blessing after another. For the law was given through Moses; grace and truth came through Jesus Christ" (John 1:16-17). Jesus Christ a unique Son of the Father full of truth and righteousness.

Jesus Christ clothes all the believers with His righteousness. In the Old Testament we have measure of grace through the Old Covenant, but in the promises of forgiveness through Jesus Christ's grace and truth are available to the fullest extent. Truth is no longer prevailed through the types of our sacrifices. Grace and truth brought blessings upon blessings, one blessing on top of another blessing. There is always a constant impartation of grace and power which has been given to all believers who responded to the grace give to them. In the gift of grace to salvation, God the Father makes all efforts to show His love to all His created beings. God the Father makes it possible and simple for all the people of this world to receive the grace of God to salvation through Jesus Christ in our Lord's redemptive work.

All true believers receive from Jesus Christ's fullness; the best and the greatest believing Christians cannot live without Him and believers have received grace for grace. All those who belong to Jesus Christ who are receiving by Christ are all summed up in this one word - grace so great a gift, and so rich, so valuable in which believers received nothing less than grace from Jesus Christ. The blessing received is grace; the goodwill of God the Father towards believers is grace and the good work of God in the life of believers is grace. Therefore, Christ is the consummation of peace and the gift of God from God the Father through Jesus Christ our Lord and Savior. It is not our works, so that no one should boast; it is purely the gift of God for salvation of all His creatures.

"My shield is God most high, who saves the upright in heart. God is a righteous judge, a God who expresses His wrath every day. If He does not relent, He will sharpen His sword; He will bend and string His bow. He has prepared His deadly weapons; He makes ready His flaming arrows. I will give thanks to the Lord because of His righteousness and will sing praise to the name of the Lord Most High" (Psalm 7:10-13,17). *The Holy Spirit teaches that the righteous can expect God to deliver and help them in times of affliction. Believers may appeal to God on the basis of a clear conscience and their sincere endeavor to maintain uprightness of heart.*

Chapter 7

Christ the Consummation of Peace in Righteousness

Christians must always expect the righteousness of God, "You heavens above, rain down righteousness; let the clouds shower it down, let the Earth open wide, let salvation spring up, let righteousness grow with it; I the Lord, have created it" (Isaiah 45:8). A day will come in the history of this world that all the nations will acknowledge that the God of Israel is the only God - the Holy Trinity - Father, Son and the Holy Spirit and He will never again be put to shame.

All the believers must not expect salvation without righteousness, they are bound up together and the Lord created them together. Jesus Christ died to save people from their sins, not in their sins; He made redemption to believers by being made to believer's righteousness and sanctification. This great deliverance of believers from their sin is from Heaven, and if all the believers open their hearts to receive this righteousness, it will produce the fruits of righteousness and great salvation.

The Scripture revealed, "I, the Lord, have called you in righteousness; I will take hold of your hand. I will keep you and will make you to be a covenant for the people and a light for the Gentiles. It pleases the Lord for the sake of His righteousness to make His Law great and glorious" (Isaiah 42:6, 21). The Messiah's mission will include bringing the covenant of the salvation of God to the Gentiles as well as the Jews according to the prophesy of Prophet Isaiah. The New Covenant will be established by the death of the Messiah, by His death and the power of the Holy Spirit, the Messiah will free all believers from the power of darkness of sin and guilt and release them from the power and from the dominion of Satan.

Prophet Isaiah continued His prophecies: "The fruit of righteousness will be peace; the effect of righteousness will be quietness and confidence forever" (Isaiah 32:17). Isaiah affirmed that the righteousness and blessings of the Kingdom will come when the Holy Spirit will be poured out from Heaven on God's people and their descendants. Today we see that the blessing of redemption comes to believers through the Holy Spirit, who has been poured out upon them from the Day of Pentecost. The out pouring of the Holy Spirit is not yet complete; believers are waiting for and praying for the fullness of redemption and the out pouring of the Holy Spirit at the end of the age.

God the Father Almighty is the fountain of all that exists and therefore He is the fountain of all power. It is the Messiah's responsibility and His commission given Him by God the Father to show that the work of redemption was complete, in the nature with the people of the world to the allegiance they owe to God as their Creator. God gave the Messiah His full presence and He was called by God. When an angel was sent from Heaven to strengthen Him in the garden in His agonies, the Father Himself was right there with Him, and this promise was fulfilled.

God who freely gave us Jesus Christ, gave believers all the blessings of the New Covenant. There are two glorious blessings from God the Father in Jesus Christ. His Gospel that also brings the Gentiles light and liberty. Jesus Christ was the light of the people of this world by His Spirit in the Word. He presents the word of the Gospel by His Spirit in the heart. He prepares the organ and He was sent to proclaim liberty to the captives, and He did by His grace.

Jesus Christ is the consummation of peace in righteousness as the Scripture revealed: "The Spirit

Himself testifies with our spirit that we are God's children. Now if we are children, then we are heirs - heirs of God and co-heirs with Christ, if indeed we share in His sufferings in order that we may also share in His glory" (Romans 8:16-17). The Holy Spirit imparted to believers a word of confidence that says - through Christ and with Christ, we are God's children.

The Spirit of God in Jesus Christ makes it clear and reveals the truth that Christ loved believers and that He still loves them and lives forever for them in Heaven as a mediator and as an intercessor. The Spirit also shows believers clearly that the Father loves all the believers as His adopted children, no less than He loves His begotten Son. Christ loves all those who belong to Him and gives them His righteousness. When God sees believers, He sees Christ's own righteousness in them. The Holy Spirit created in all those who believe in Jesus Christ love and confidence by which in any trouble or affliction, they may be able to cry out to Him. Jesus Christ suffered for all believing Christians, therefore we must also suffer with Him; it is the consequence of our relationship with the Father as His children, our identification with Christ, and God the Father, as His children, our witness for Him and our refusal to conform to the world.

Many people in this world speak peace to themselves to whom the God of Heaven does not speak peace, but those who are sanctified have God's spirit witnessing with their spirits. This is really and always in agreement with the Word of God and it is therefore always grounded upon sanctification. The Holy Spirit's activities did not extend to those who are not the children of God; the privileges of the children will not extend to those who do not have the nature and disposition of children of God. The happiness of all the believers is in the future glory. In the earthly inheritances, this rule does not hold, only the first-born are called heirs to the inheritance.

Believers did not come to it by any merit of their own, or by any work of their own; but as heirs, purely by the activities of God before the foundation of the world. The believers' present state is a state of lecturing and preparing them for their heavenly inheritance. All true believers shall inherit all things that are for those that are now partakers of His glory. The future glory of believers is the rewards of their suffering with Christ.

All the believing Christians must be: "Filled with the fruit of righteousness that comes through Jesus Christ to the glory and praise of God" (Philippians 1:11). All the believing Christians must have a full commitment to the

Lord Jesus Christ and to God's Word and His will; they must be pure and blameless full of righteousness until the day of Jesus Christ. The fruit of righteousness is from God and therefore, from it must be asked that believers must not have fear of being emptied to bring forth the fruits of righteousness, for they will always be filled. These fruits are by Jesus Christ and they are unto the glory and praises of God.

All the believing Christians must focus on doing good works. Apostle Paul said: "Now there is in store for me the crown of righteousness, which the Lord, the righteous judge, will award to me on that day and not only me, but also to all who have longed for His appearing" (2nd Timothy 4:8). When believers remain faithful to the Lord and to the Gospel service entrusted to them, the Holy Spirit will witness to them that God's loving approval and the crown of righteousness will be waiting for them in Heaven. God Almighty has reserved His rewards in Heaven for all who remain loyal to Jesus Christ and His Gospel.

All the believing Christians are longing to live with Jesus Christ their Lord and Savior in Heaven one day. "And to put on the new self, created to be like God in true righteousness and holiness" (Ephesians4:24). Believers receive a new nature; they are new creature. New believers were created by God's mighty power. Believers must produce fruits that will bring glory to God, and happiness that comes from the new man, which is righteousness towards people around them in the world and holiness towards God their creator. We can see and come to the clear conclusion that Jesus Christ is the consummation of peace in righteousness to those who believe and give their lives to Jesus Christ in singleness of heart and in true holiness and righteousness. Le all the believing Christians offer sacrifices of praise that the fruit of our lips give to Him thankfulness and prayer for His righteousness towards His creation. He is a righteous God and Judge, full of righteousness and mercy.

All those who believe in Jesus Christ and gave their lives to Him, God credited them with the righteousness that Jesus Christ purchased with His precious blood on the Cross. God deposited to the believers' account as a gift of Christ's righteousness that when God sees a converted sinner, He sees that they were imputed with Christ's righteousness in that believers have been clothed in the righteousness of Jesus Christ. From then on they have peace with God, as well as access to God because in Jesus Christ believers are now adopted children of God and co-heir with Jesus Christ.

As the Scripture says, "Dear friends, now we are children of God and what we will be has not yet been made known. But we know that when He appears, we shall be like Him, for we shall see Him as He is" (1st John 3:2). Believers have the nature of the children of God by regeneration. The glory of the children of God and adoption has been reserved for the new earth where only the righteous will dwell. Believers must walk by faith as well as live by hope. The children of God will be known and they will be made manifest by their likeness of Jesus Christ. Their likeness is that they shall be like Jesus Christ, they shall have Him and they shall see His smile and the beauty of His face. Their likeness shall enable them to see Him as the blessed in Heaven. Believing Christians will be sanctified by faith, and they must be sanctified by hope, so that they may be saved by hope and purified by hope because hope does not disappoint.

"So the wall was completed on the twenty-fifth of Elul, in fifty-two days. When all our enemies heard about this, all the surrounding nations were afraid and lost their self-confidence, because they realized that this work had been done with the help of our God" (Nehemiah 6:15-16). The reason why the wall was completed is because God Almighty was with His people because they were courageous, dedicated and a persevering leader, Nehemiah, depended fully on God as His protection and as the source of His strength.

Chapter 8

Christ the Consummation of Peace of the Resurrection

Jesus Christ is the only consummation of peace in resurrection. The Scripture revealed that: "On the first day of the week, very early in the morning, the women took the spices they had prepared and went to the tomb. They found that the stone rolled away from the tomb, but when they entered, they did not find the body of the Lord Jesus Christ. While they were wondering about this, suddenly two men in clothes that gleamed like lighting stood beside them... 'Why do you look for the living among the dead? He is not here; He has risen!' " (Luke 24:1-6). The angel told the women that came to the tomb with spices that Jesus Christ has risen.

Christ's resurrection has been confirmed by so many scriptural facts. (a) It confirmed the empty tomb. If the Lord's enemies had taken His body from the tomb, they would have displayed it to prove that He had not risen from the dead. On the other hand, if His disciples had taken His body, they would have never sacrificed their lives and possessions for what they knew to be untrue. The empty tomb reveals that Jesus Christ did arise and truly was the true Son of God. (b) Jesus Christ shows His existence, His power, His joy, His dedication and devotion to the early church. If Jesus Christ had not risen and appeared to them, they would have never changed from deep sorrow, despair of sorrow and the loss of hope in their Lord to unheard of joy, courage and hope. But Jesus Christ is the consummation of peace because on the day of resurrection He brought joy to the heart of all the apostles and all the believers today.

The New Testament was written by the apostles and men who witness the resurrection of Jesus Christ and willingly gave their lives for the truth and the righteous teaching during Christ's Earthly ministry. They would never have taken the trouble to write about the Messiah - and His teaching if His ministry ended when He died on the Cross. The Scripture revealed: "But if it is preached that Christ has been raised from the dead, how can some of you say there is no resurrection of the dead? If there is no resurrection of the dead, then not even Christ has been raised. And if Christ has not been raised, our preaching is useless and so is your faith. More than that, we are then found to be false witnesses about God, for we have testified about God that He raised Christ from the dead. But He did not raise Him if in fact the dead are not raised, and then Christ has not been raised either. And if Christ has not been raised, your faith is futile; you are still in your sins. Then those also who have fallen asleep in Christ are lost. If only for this life we have hope in Christ we are to be pitied more than all men. For since death came through a man, the resurrection of the dead comes also through a man. For as in Adam all die, so in Christ all will be made alive" (1st Corinthians 15:12-22).

This fact of the Scriptures shows clearly that Jesus Christ has been raised from the dead to the glory of God the Father. If those who say that our resurrection is false hope are right in their accusation, then, that means the entire Christian life is based on a fraud, and even if we feel that we are happy we might feel miserable on the other hand, as some people who deny Christ's bodily resurrection. Paul the apostle states clearly that if Christ has not been raised, then there is no deliverance from sin. Therefore, those who deny the objective reality of the resurrection of Jesus Christ are denying the Christians' faith altogether. They are false witnesses who speak against God and His Word. Those peoples' faith is worthless and useless; they are not, therefore, authentic Christian believers.

Christ Jesus' consummation of resurrection brought the baptism in the Holy Spirit and His accompanying manifestation with the Church. The Holy Spirit was poured out at the Day of Pentecost as an experiential reality proof that Jesus Christ had risen and was exalted at the right hand of God in Heaven. If Jesus Christ had not risen, there would have been no experience of baptism in the Holy Spirit. The Scripture revealed: "But I tell you the truth: it is for your good that I am going away. Unless I go away; the counselor will not come to you; but if I go, I will send him to you" (John 16:7). Jesus Christ was speaking of the Pentecostal out pouring of the Holy Spirit, which Christ said, it can only happen after He goes back to Heaven. Therefore, the Scripture said: "After His suffering, He showed Himself to these men and gave many convincing proofs that He was alive. He appeared to them over a period of forty days and spoke about the Kingdom of God. On one occasion, while He was eating with them, He gave them this command: 'Do not leave Jerusalem, but wait for the gift my Father promised, which you have heard me speak about. For John baptized with water, but in a few days you will be baptized with the Holy Spirit" (Acts 1:3-5).

Christ's resurrection brought joy and peace to the people of this world. Christ appeared to His disciples in numerous occasions for the period of forty-days to prove that He was alive. The Scripture revealed: "So the women hurried away from the tomb, afraid and filled with joy, and ran to tell His disciples. Suddenly Jesus met them. 'Greetings,' he said. They came to him, clasped his feet and worshiped him. Then Jesus said to them. 'Do not be afraid.' Go and tell my brothers to go to Galilee; there they will see me" (Matthew 28:8-10). The resurrection of Jesus Christ is well verified historically. After His resurrection, Jesus Christ remained on this Earth for many days, appearing and talking to the apostles and many of His followers.

The resurrection of Jesus Christ's appearances are as follows - Jesus Christ appeared to Mary Magdalene; He appeared to women returning from the tomb; Christ appeared to Peter; He appeared to the two travelers on the road to Emmaus; He appeared to all the disciples at once except Thomas Didymus and all others with them; Christ appeared to all the disciples on Sunday night one week later. Christ appeared to seven disciples by the sea of

Galilee; He also appeared to five hundred people in Galilee with James His brother; Christ appeared to the disciples receiving the Great Commission - Christ with the apostles and all His followers on the day of His ascension and finally Christ appeared to Apostle Paul and strengthened him before they took him to Rome. The angel told the women do not be afraid, that they brought good news of resurrection of Jesus Christ to them. In the same way, the angels brought the good news of Christ's birth to the world.

The women were very loyal to Jesus Christ; they remained steadfast and immovable friends of Jesus Christ when the rest of the people in the world despised and crucified Him. The baptism in the Holy Spirit is the fulfillment of the promise of God the Father which we describe as being filled with the Holy Spirit, baptized in the Holy Spirit and filled with the Spirit are used interchangeably. Jesus Christ Himself is the one who baptized those who believe in Him in the Holy Spirit. The primary purpose of baptism in the Holy Spirit is to receive power to witness for Christ so that the sinners and the lost will be converted to Him and they will be able to be taught how to obey all that Jesus commanded. The resurrection of Jesus Christ brought the consummation of peace to the world.

The resurrection of Jesus Christ is a testimony to the general resurrection of all human beings, which will be followed by the dispensation of God's justice to the righteous. There will be a resurrection of condemnation. Jesus Christ's bodily resurrection is the basis for all the humanity's future resurrection. The gift that was given after Christ's resurrection which is the Holy Spirit is the guarantee, or first installment that shows that God the Father will raise all the righteous people in the world from the dead if they give their life to Him through faith in Jesus Christ, His only begotten Son. All believers must make all efforts to please God and believe in His Word.

"Ezra opened the book. All the people could see Him because He was standing above them; and as He opened it, the people all stood up. Ezra praised the Lord, the great God; and all the people lifted their hands and responded. Amen! Amen! Then they bowed down and worshiped the Lord with their faces to the ground" *(Nehemiah 8:5-6). This is one of the greatest worship services and is one of its kind from the children of Israel. God the Father desires the adoration of His people and He calls all the people in all the nations of Earth to worship Him regularly.*

Chapter 9

Christ the Consummation of Peace of Eternal Life

We first read about the eternal God in the Book of Genesis: "Abraham planted a tamarisk tree in Beersheba, and there He called upon the name of the Lord, the Eternal God" (Genesis 21:33) Abraham worship and called Him God Eternal in His prayers. The Scripture revealed also that "The eternal God is your refuge, and underneath are the everlasting arms. He will drive out your enemy before you, saying, destroy Him!" (Deuteronomy 33:27). Abraham stayed in Philistine for many days; there He made, not only constant practice of prayers to God, but He made an open confession of His relationship with God. He built a house of prayer to prove His love for God. Christ prayed in a garden, on a mountain, calling on His Father, we Christians believers must follows the footsteps of Abraham and our Lord Jesus Christ, and call unto Him daily as long as we are on this Earth.

In calling on the Lord, we must put our trust in Him as the everlasting Lord. Our everlasting God who was, before all worlds and will be when the time and the days shall be no more. "You have made known to me the path of life; you will fill me with joy in your presence with eternal pleasures at your right hand" "Surely you have granted eternal blessings and made Him glad with the joy of your presence." "The fear of the Lord is the beginning of wisdom; all who follow His precepts have good understanding. To Him belongs eternal praise"(Psalm 16:11, 21:6, 111:10).

The psalmist trusted in the Lord, and believed that after death, He is going to where He will enjoy the blessings of God's presence. God will also redeem His life from the grave and take them to Himself in Heaven. We Christian believers must believe in eternal life, which Jesus Christ offered to those who believe in Him. We see from the Old Testament how people believe in spending eternal life in God's presence with joy. All the believing Christians need to praise the Lord for His physical and for His spiritual blessings as well as for His providential care over those who love the Lord and fear Him.

People of this Earth must determine to praise the Lord not privately in the corner of their rooms, but also in the church, gathering places, in the assembly. It is Scriptural to give unceasing praises to God Almighty spontaneously and with a loud voice in the church. This truth should serve as a foundation for the Old Testament wisdom of God and for the New Testament wisdom of Jesus Christ's eternal life, which He offered to the people of this world. "All your words are time; all your righteous laws are eternal" (Psalm 119:160). The Lord is near to all those who love Him and to all those who love His Word. If any believers are going through some problems, such as illness, afflictions, distresses, they must pick their Bible and read the Word of God so that the Holy Spirit will revive their spirit, soul and body so that their relationship with God will be energized, restored, and strengthen them; Christ will be able to help them in so many ways they cannot imagine through His eternal spirit drawing them nearer to Himself and comfort their soul as well as blesses them immeasurably.

Where the fear of the Lord rules in the heart there will be a constant conscientious care to deep His commandments, not to talk of them only, but to do them; and such have a good understanding. The believers' obedience is a plain indication of their mind that they do, indeed fear the Lord. All the believing Christians have many reasons to offer praises and thankfulness to God, to praise Him forever for His mercy and love, putting man into such a fair and love way to happiness from this Earth to Heaven.

Believers must thank God for the faithfulness of His Word. Since the beginning of creation when God began to reveal Himself to the people of this world, to the children of Israel, all He said was true and God's Word are to be trusted. The church from the beginning was built upon the rock, which is God's Word. It has never lost His value, but the beginning of the Word of God is true and valid. It was laid on the sure foundation, and it continues to be found in faith to the end. "Trust in the Lord forever, for the Lord, the Lord, is the Rock Eternal" (Isaiah 26:4). God will keep in perfect peace the remnant that remains steadfast and faithful to their Lord.

In times of trouble believers must continually strive to keep their minds turned to the Lord in prayer, believers must trust and hope in the Lord. They must place their trust in Him because He is the rock who endures forever. He is a sure and firm foundation. Eternal life is in Jesus Christ as the consummation of peace. All who belong to Jesus Christ are safe; they have security of mind in the assurance of God's favor. God will keep them in perfect peace, and in inward peace, and outward peace, peace with God, peace of conscience and peace under any circumstances in the world.

Those that trust in the Lord must have their minds stayed upon Him and such are those that God the Father will keep in perpetual peace, and that peace shall keep them. They will trust the Lord forever, at all times. Whatever we trust in the world will last for a short time; it is confined within the limits of time. But when we trust God with our lives, it will last as long as we shall live on Earth because Christ is the One who was, and who is, and who is to come. He is the rock of ages, a firm and lasting foundation for believers' faith that is built upon Him and He is the house built on a rock that stands forever in any storms of life - Jesus Christ is the rock of our life. Jesus Christ said: "And everyone who has left houses or brothers or sisters or father for my sake will receive a hundred times as much and will inherit eternal life" (Matthew 19:29). The Scripture revealed that those who do not want to know God, or keep His commandment will be punished: "Then they will go away to eternal punishment, but the righteous to eternal life" (Matthew 25:46). Our Lord Jesus Christ teaches that the wicked and evildoers shall go into everlasting punishment while the righteous shall go into life eternal; it means they shall inherit the Kingdom. Heaven is life where there is happiness, and where the righteous people eternally live with God.

There is no death to put time to the life and neither there is old age to put a period of old age, it is a place of comfort; there is no sorrow, no bitterness, there is no good or bad, no evil, no blessing and no curse are set before them that they may choose from, no death no suffering there eternal life cannot compare to anything on Earth. Let all believers give thanks to Jesus Christ for His blessing of eternal life. In the most popular Scripture about eternal life: "For God so loved the world that He gave His one and only Son, that whoever believes in Him shall not perish but have eternal life" (John 3:16). In John 3:16, the great Gospel mystery revealed; John was telling believers about the heart of God and the purpose of God in all His creations.

God's love is so wide enough to embrace all the people in the world. God the Father gave His one and only begotten Son as an offering for our sin on the Cross. The atonement proceeds from the loving heart of God. It was not something forced on Him. Those who believe in Jesus Christ must have a sure conviction that He is the Son of God and the Savior of all the people in the world.

Believers must be completely surrendered to the fellowship and lordship with obedience to Jesus Christ's commands. Eternal life will be giving to who are fully trusted in Jesus Christ that He is both able and willing to bring them their final salvation and fellowship with God in Heaven. Eternal life is the gift that God the Father Almighty bestowed on the believers when they are born again; it means when they turn their life to Jesus Christ.

Eternal life expresses perpetuity, but also a quality of divine life; a life that frees believers from what is merely an earthly order for them to be able to know God. Jesus Christ is the only begotten Son of God - God loves us so much that He gave His only begotten Son to the people of this Earth. It pleases God the Father to give His only Son for the redemption and the salvation of humankind. He gave Him up to suffer and die for the sin of humanity on the Cross. In this way, we see how God the Father has commended His love to the people of the world. This shows how God really loved the world so richly to include both the Jews and the Gentiles through Jesus Christ there is a general offer of life and salvation, which was made to all the people in the world.

God sent His Son to the world with a proposal, that whosoever believes in Jesus shall never perish or die; Jesus

Christ is known as the offer of salvation - the Gospel duty is that people must believe in Jesus Christ. The great Gospel blessing is that whosoever believes in Jesus Christ will have eternal life. God has taken away their sin; they have been wash clean with the blood of the Lamb and they shall not perish at the second death; a pardon is purchased for them. Jesus Christ has paid for their sin; they are now entitled to the joys of Heaven to have an eternal life in Heaven forever.

It is God's desire and it is God's plan before the creation of the world in sending His Son into the world so that the world through Him might be saved. Jesus Christ came to the world with the salvation of God in His hand and with peace; He is the consummation of the world peace. "Whoever believes in the Son has eternal life, but whoever rejects the Son will not see life, for God's wrath remains on Him" (John 3:36). The Gospel of God comes as a free gift, but the believer accepted it. It will not leave them to do as they please which means they cannot go back, and live a life of sin. It requires that they enter into the way of salvation ordained by God and they must be subjected to the way of righteousness of God.

Our Lord had a conversation with the woman in the well; the Samaritan woman: "Jesus answered, everyone who drinks this water will be thirsty again; but whoever drinks the water I give Him will never thirst. Indeed, the water I give Him will become in Him a spring of water welling up to eternal life" (John 4:14). Jesus Christ told the Samaritan woman about eternal life; Jesus Christ at the time of His conversation with the Samaritan woman, reveals His commitment to His heavenly Father's purpose and His own inner desire to bring people to eternal life. Jesus Christ shows His great passion and desire was to save the lost. Believers must follow Christ's footsteps to develop a passion and desire to save the sinners and the lost around them.

People are ready to hear God's Word; we must find ways to speak to them about their spiritual need and about Jesus Christ, who is ready to solve all their problems, provides for their needs. The water that Jesus was explaining to the Samaritan woman is a spiritual life. People of this Earth must partake of this living water; they must drink it. This act of drinking is not a momentary, single or one time activity, but rather it is a progressive or repeated drinking. Drinking the water of life requires regular communion with the source of the living water, Jesus Christ Himself.

No one can continue to drink the water of life without getting close to the source such people will become "Springs without water" (2nd Peter 2:17). All the believers must be devoted Christians. Our Lord Jesus said, "Even now the reaper draws His wages, even now He harvests the crop for eternal life, so that the sower and the reaper may be glad together" (John 4:36). Jesus teaches that those who bring others to saving faith in Jesus Christ are doing something of eternal consequences. They will one day rejoice in Heaven over those who were saved because of their prayers and witnesses. At the same time, they must understand that their work is often a reaping of the labors of others such like the work of the apostles.

"Nehemiah said. 'Go and enjoy choice food and sweet drinks, and send some to those who have nothing prepared. This day is sacred to our Lord. Do not grieve, for the joy of the Lord is your strength' " (Nehemiah 8:10). The declaration of God's Word, accompanied by a sincere desire to follow its instruction, will result in a true, heartfelt joy. The "Joy of the Lord" is based on reconciliation with God and the presence of the Spirit in our lives. The joy of the Lord is maintained by the assurance that the believer has been forgiven in Christ and restored to fellowship with God, and that they are now live in good harmony with His will.

Chapter 10

Christ the Consummation of Peace
of the Holy Spirit

The Scripture revealed how Jesus Christ promised disciples about the Holy Spirit: "And I will ask the Father, and He will give you another counselor to be with you forever - the Spirit of Truth. The world cannot accept him because it neither sees him nor knows him. But you know him, for he lives with you and will be in you. I will not leave you as orphans; I will come to you" (John 14:16-18). Jesus Christ during His teaching and preaching told the apostles to ask in His name in prayer anything they needed; if they pray according to His Will. Jesus said that He will ask the Father for what they needed to live for Him forever.

Jesus Christ is our great intercessor in Heaven. He intercedes for us at the right hand of God the Father when we are going through difficulties for what we need. Jesus said He will ask the Father to give every believing Christian the Counselor to only those who are serious about their love for Him and their devotion to His Word. Christ emphasizes the spirit of love and obedience. The Counselor, the Holy Spirit will be indwelling the believers and help them to live a Christians life. The Holy Spirit strengthens believers and empowers them to teach and preach and witness the Gospel to other people in the world; The Holy Spirit will comfort them during any time of difficulties and in any situation.

The Holy Spirit will intercede in prayer for believers; the prayer that cannot be uttered which will be between Him and God. The Holy Spirit will serve as a best friend in order for believers to further their best interest and remain faithful forever with Christ. The Holy Spirit is the Spirit of truth. He will communicate the truth of the Gospel through believers to non-believers. From the beginning of creation, the Spirit of God was involved with the creation of the Earth. God Almighty had specific reasons for creating the world; He created the heavens and Earth for the manifestation of His glory, wisdom and power. He created the heavens and the Earth in order to receive by worship His glory and honor. All God's creations such as the stars, the sun, the moon, and other planets, mountains forest trees, rain, snow, volcanoes, hurricane, storms, rivers, oceans and all the creatures in the ocean, such as: animals, birds and all creatures that crawl on the ground, the tiny aunts, and flies, everything seen and unseen, they acknowledge their existent through God, giving praise, honor and giving Him all the praise due Him.

The Lord Jesus Christ said: "I tell you, He replied, if they keep quiet, the stones will cry out." (Luke 19:40). God requires a fellowship and communication through prayers from all believing Christians. The Scripture revealed that God is an infinite, self-existent and He always existed even before He created the Earth and all other planets: "In the beginning God created the heavens and the Earth. Now the Earth was formless and empty darkness was over the surface of the deep, and the Spirit of God was hovering over the waters" (Genesis 1:1-2). The Spirit of God is hovering telling us the role of the Holy Spirit before the beginning of creation. Since God is the source of all that exists from human beings and nature not self-existent, but they owed their being and their continuance to God.

All existence and life is dependent on Him; all life and creation are eternally meaningful and all are purposeful. God Almighty has a sovereign right over all creation by His virtue of being their Creator. The consummation of the Holy Trinity opened wide when Jesus Christ came to the world in human form. The Spirit of God in creation became the spirit incarnation, crucified, and raised to life. The Spirit of the Lord Jesus Christ is the inclusive compound and life-giving Spirit that makes the believers to be one in Him and alive. Now Jesus Christ is the Emmanuel God in us and God dwelling in us; Jesus Christ is with us living His life through every believer and being a Wonderful Counselor and a comforter, who also guides all the believers in all things. The Holy Spirit is available now and can be enjoyed and experienced in various ways: He is our teacher, as well as telling us what is going to happen before it happens; showing us what the Father and Son have for us before we receive it.

The Scripture revealed: "Again Jesus said, 'Peace be with you! As the Father has sent me, I am sending you.' And with that He breathed on them and said, 'Receive the Holy Spirit. If you forgive anyone His sins, they are forgiven, if you do not forgive them, they are not forgiven" (John 20:21-22). Jesus Christ breathed on the disciples and said to them receive the Holy Spirit, doing, or saying this, He made them spiritually alive, just as the Father after He formed Adam from the dust, He breathed on Him the breath of life and He became a living being. The Holy Spirit had an active role in the work of creation, hovering over the Earth, which means preserving the Earth, watching out, and monitoring the Earth as well as preparing it for what God is going to do in His activities on Earth.

The Holy Spirit continues to get involved in sustaining the creation up till this moment. The Spirit of God which is now the Holy Spirit, the life giving at the resurrection of Jesus Christ as well as the transcending ascension of Jesus Christ sitting at the right hand of God. The Holy Spirit is all-inclusive, life giving compound, profound the Spirit of Jesus Christ, the life giving Spirit, the seven Spirits of the Church. When we give our life to Jesus Christ, we receive the Holy Spirit. It dwells in all the believers of Jesus Christ and becomes the streams of living water flowing from our inner most being. Jesus said during His earthly ministry: "Whoever believes in me, as the Scripture has said, streams of living water will flow from within Him." By this He meant the Spirit, whom those who believed in Him were later to receive. Up to that time the Spirit had not been given, since Jesus had not yet been glorified" (John 7:38-39). Jesus Christ referred to the Scripture because it was the word of the Father and therefore, the supreme authority for His life and for His teaching biblically. It is also the supreme authority for all the believing Christians, for God alone has the right to determine our standards of conduct. God has chosen to exercise this authority by making His truth known in His Word.

The Bible, is God's revelation, it carries the same authority as if God Himself speaking directly to us. The inspired Scriptural Word of God is the believer's ultimate authority. To profess equal or greater allegiance to any other authority than to God and His inspired Word is to remove oneself from the biblical faith and from the Lordship of Jesus Christ. When the believer receives the gift of the Holy Spirit, they will experience His over flowing life. The living water will flow out from deep within the believer to others with the healing message of Jesus Christ.

Jesus Christ's glory is the result of His death and His resurrection; the Holy Spirit cannot be fully manifest until sin is dealt with completely. The Spirit's activities are all the work of the Holy Spirit in the life of believing Christian's regeneration and baptism of the Holy Spirit. The Scripture revealed: "Those controlled by the sinful nature cannot please God. You, however, are controlled not by the sinful nature but by the Spirit, if the Spirit of God lives in you. And if anyone does not have the Spirit of

Christ, He does not belong to Christ. But if Christ is in you, your body is dead because of sin, yet your Spirit is alive because of righteousness" (Romans 8:8-10). If any believer lives according to the sinful nature, they will die spiritually; but if they live by the Spirit, put to death all the misdeeds of the body, they will be eternally alive with God because they will be alive spiritually.

All the believing Christians from the moment of their spiritual birth and faith in Jesus Christ; they have the spirit the Holy Spirit also known as the Spirit of Christ living inside them. The indwelling presence of the Holy Spirit is related to the new birth, which is the baptism in the Holy Spirit an empowering experience that related to the initiation into the gift of the Holy Spirit. The Holy Spirit is the Holy trinity - Father, Son and the Holy Spirit the trinity has become one, forever on God with the consummated of peace and the matured transformation - transforming all those who gave their life to Jesus Christ to be able to worship God, approach the throne of grace with confidence.

The Scripture says: "The Spirit and the bride say, come. And let them who hears say, Come! Whoever is thirsty, let them come; whoever wishes, let Him take the free gift of the water of life" (Revelation 22:17). The Holy

Spirit is continuously inspiring the believers of Jesus Christ, the bride which means the church which also means the body of Christ to witness, invite all the people in the world to the salvation of Jesus Christ. The Holy Spirit has empowered, and inspired the Church, which is the body of Christ by the Spirit to proclaim the Gospel, the testimony of Jesus Christ to all the people in the world until Christ returns to Earth to judge the quick and the dead and all eyes shall see Him.

Until then we urge all the Christian believers to make their priority goal to reach the sinners and the lost for Jesus Christ in so many ways possible with the power of the Holy Spirit; we must consummate with the Holy Spirit in everything we do for Jesus Christ in the work of the ministry, and as well as in the service of the Holy Trinity forever one God. Believing Christians must rejoice in the Lord worship Him with the Spirit of holiness from this Earth to Heaven.

The Holy Spirit is involved with the work of Jesus Christ new Heaven and new Earth; Jesus Christ will make sure that the consummation of salvation in the lives all the glorified believers are in place. Holy Spirit will transform believer's body from mortally to immortality. The true body of Christ; the church will be completed, assembled together as well as glorified with Jesus Christ. The Earth and all other planets will experience Jesus Christ redemptive through the Holy Spirit's transformation work. The universe will be restored back to its original purity just as when Adam and Eve were first created and they were living there without sin. It will become eternal paradise of God. God will live among His people. All the people who will be in the new Earth will worship God the Father, God the Son, and God the Holy Spirit forever.

"Stand up and praise the Lord your God, who is from everlasting to everlasting. Blessed be your glorious name, and may it be exalted above all blessing and praise. You alone are the Lord. You made the heavens, even the highest heavens, and all their starry host, the Earth and all that is on it, the seas and all that is in them. You give life to everything, and the multitudes of Heaven worship you" (Nehemiah 9:5b-6). *Believing Christians' main goal is to offer prayer to God for His gracious endeavor and provision of redemption and His salvation to the people of Israel and to the Gentiles; throughout history His divine love never has never failed.*

Chapter 11

Christ the Consummation of Peace of our Salvation

The consummation of all the believing Christians to salvation is in three ways: (a) Christ came to this world; He died for sinners, like me. Jesus Christ was buried and raised to life on the third day and He ascended to Heaven. (b) He begins His second ministry when He arrived in Heaven and is seated at the right hand of God, interceding and praying for us. Jesus Christ's earthly ministry consisted of what He did for us, the agony of the crucifixion on the Cross and His resurrection. When Christ was crucified all believers were crucified, when He was raised to life, all the believers were raised to life. He was raised in a glorious body. Christ the sacrificial Lamb of God brings peace between God and man. Jesus Christ, the indwelling Lord and Savior gives all believers the peace of God, a fruit of the Holy Spirit. Peace with God means divine relationship between His created beings.

All the enmity between man and God was removed permanently. Jesus Christ becomes the transformer; His transformation process in the lives of those who believe in Him is very amazing, miraculous and powerful. The heavenly ministry of Jesus Christ is if a person repents and has faith in Him, and were baptized, they enter into Christ, and Christ enters into them; they become born again by the Spirit of God; they are new believers and they have a new standing before God. A new believer immediately enters into the benefits of Christ's heavenly ministry where they totally surrender to the lordship of Jesus Christ as well as permitting Jesus Christ to transform their life.

The Scripture revealed: "Jesus has been found worthy of greater honor than Moses, just as the builder of a house has greater honor that the house itself. For every house is built by someone, but God is the builder of everything" (Hebrews 3:3-4). Jesus Christ is superior to any religious system. The author of the Book of Hebrews uses an important sentence when He said, "Which has greater honor, the builder of a house or the house? The answer is the builder. He is the one that has more honor than the house. Jesus Christ has more honor than anyone else in the universe, as a creator of the Earth; He actually designed and made all the people in the world. Jesus Christ deserves all our respect and all our allegiance; by becoming human. Jesus Christ learned obedience, temptation, and sufferings that people of this Earth go through, in order to be able to represent believers sympathetically to God.

Jesus Christ is higher than Moses, Aaron, the High Priest and all the prophets. Jesus Christ is the Messiah, Jesus our Savior and our healer. Jesus Christ is the gift of grace from God the Father, and He is the Spirit of grace that came down from Heaven. He brought Heaven into the soul of all the humanity. Moses was faithful in the discharge of His office in the Old Testament, and in the same way Jesus Christ under the New Testament was superior to Moses. The superior glory and excellence of Jesus Christ was above and beyond Moses. Christ Jesus was the maker of His own house, Christ, who is God, drew the foundation and plan of His Church, provided the materials, and disposed them in order to receive the form; Christ united His house, and crowned all with His own presence, which is the true glory of this house of God. Jesus Christ was the master of His house as well as the maker - Moses was only a faithful servant. Jesus Christ, as the eternal Son of God, is the rightful owner and the Sovereign ruler of the Church which is His body. Jesus

Christ is more worthy and of more glory than Moses; Christ is of greater regard and consideration.

Jesus Christ is fulfilling all the Old Testament requirements. Jesus Christ was the Priest who could permanently bring God and man together as God the Son; He has the power through His death and resurrection to remove the final barrier of sin between God and all the humanity. God the Father Almighty shows many ways to reveals Himself; through His creations, through the prophets, but now finally, complete self-expression through His Son Jesus Christ the one and only that is worthy of all honor and glory. Because of Jesus Christ righteousness, believers will no longer approach God through a Priest, as the people of Israel. Christ Jesus work of redemption makes God available to all who have faith in Him. God no longer lives in a designed temple; believers have become God's house and God's temple because our heart is the temple of the Holy Spirit, which dwells in us.

God the Father is now speaking to all the people of this world through His Son whom He appointed the heir of all things and through only He created the universe. Therefore, Jesus Christ our high Priest in Heaven was faithful to God the Father whom through Him He created the world. Jesus Christ is our great high Priest who has passed through the heavens, who is always sympathized with our weaknesses, and afflictions. All believers must make every effort to approach the throne of grace boldly in order to receive mercy as well as find grace in all the areas of our needs. Jesus Christ holds His Priesthood permanently and forever so that He can continue to make intercession for those who believe in Him. Jesus Christ through His precious blood is cleansing all believers so that they can worship the living God.

We need to see also Jesus Christ and Melchizedek King of Salem what the Scripture says: "And He says in another place, you are a Priest forever, in the order of Melchizedek. For it is declared: you are a Priest forever, in the order of Melchizedek." (Hebrews 5:6, 7:17) Melchizedek was a mysterious Old Testament figure who appears in the book of Genesis Chapter 14:18 - as God Priest of Salem; Jesus Christ Priesthood is the same as of Melchizedek He is a contemporary of Abraham, He was a Canaanite King of Salem and a Priest of God. Abraham paid titles to Him and He blessed Abraham. The Bible says that we should consider Melchizedek with Jesus Christ, because they were both Priest and King.

Jesus Christ's Priesthood is in the order of Melchizedek means that Jesus Christ is both before and He is greater than Abraham and all other Levitical Priests. The Levitical Priesthood was not perfect because it was administered by sinful human being. Therefore, it was replaced by the perfect Priest because He is wholly righteous, He provides a once and for all sacrifice for our sins, He serve as our eternal Priest before God in Heaven, and lives forever more. Therefore, for these reasons He is able to save completely and forever all those who come to God through Him.

The Law, by which Jesus Christ was constituted as a Priest, after the order of Melchizedek, was from the power of an endless life. This gives the preference infinitely to Jesus Christ and the Gospel. The High Priest of our profession holds His office by that inner power of endless life which He has in Himself, which He use to communicate eternal life to all those who rely upon His sacrifice and His intercession. The most important point is that the Priesthood of Jesus Christ brings along a better hope; it shows believers the true foundation of all hope that they have poses towards God for pardon and salvation. With this hope believers are encouraged to draw near unto God, they were encourage to live a life of good communion with the Lord.

Jesus Christ is the author of eternal salvation of people of the world; this salvation is bestowed on those who were obedient to His Word. Believers must hearken to the word of Jesus Christ and obey Him. He is exalted to be a price and our ruler, ruler of all the human soul on Earth as well as our Savior and deliverer; He will be our Savior to those whom He is a prince He will be the author and the finisher of their faith to salvation. The Scripture says: "Yet for us there is but one God, the Father, from whom all things came and for whom we live; and there is but one Lord, Jesus Christ, through whom all things came and through whom we live" (1st Corinthians 8:6). There is no other God but one - all the believing Christians know that is but one God. All things are of Him, and we, and every thing else, are for Him. It is a great privilege for us Christians that we know that our God, is the true God of Heaven and He is the true mediator between God and man.

The Consummation of all the believers' salvation brought a big blessing from the Father and from His Son Jesus Christ: "But our citizenship is in Heaven. And we eagerly await a Savior from there, the Lord Jesus Christ, who, by the power that enables Him to bring everything under His control, will transform our lowly bodies so that they will be like His glorious body" (Philippians 3:20-21)

All the believer's citizenship is in Heaven, Heaven is our home, our citizenship as Christians is in Heaven, not in this world, we have become strangers and aliens on the Earth. In regards to our life's walk with the Lord, our values and directions, Heaven is now our Father's land. We have been born from above, our names are written on the book of the Lamb and book of Life, our lives are guided by the heavenly standards, and our rights and inheritance are reserved in Heaven. Believers' prayers ascend straight to Heaven where Jesus sits at the right hand of God. Believers' hope is directed to Heaven - Jesus Christ is there preparing a place for us; there we will enjoy our glorified body.

the second coming of Jesus Christ we expected to be happy and glorified. There is a glory reserved for the children of God, which they will be in stated in at the resurrection, the body of believers will be made glorious body. The Scripture also mention about our heavenly body: "There are also heavenly bodies and there are Earthly bodies; but the splendor of the heavenly bodies is one kind, and the splendor of the Earthly bodies is another. The Spiritual did not come first, but the natural, and after that the spiritual. So it is written; the first man Adam became a living being, the last Adam, a life given spirit.

The first man was dust of the Earth, the second man from Heaven. And just as we have borne the likeness of the Earthly man, so shall we bear the likeness of the man from Heaven" (1st Corinthians 15: 40-47,49). All the believing Christians one day they will be in eternity, God will consummate their salvation in Christ Jesus by giving them the same body like Jesus glorious body. As there are heavenly bodies same way there are Earthly bodies, heavenly bodies will never decay or see corruption. Earthly bodies were buried in weakness, but they are going to be raised in power. Believer's Earthly bodies are natural body but they are going to be raised as a spiritual body. Believers receive glorious bodies when they are obedient to God's Word and follow His commandment.

Believer's bodies were buried in corruption, they were raised as incorruptible. The Scripture says: So will it be with the resurrection of the dead. The body that is sown is perishable, it is raised imperishable. I declare to you, brothers, that flesh and blood cannot inherit the kingdom of God, nor does the perishable inherit the imperishable. Listen, I tell you a mystery: we will not sleep, but we will all be changed; in a flash, in the twinkling of an eye, at the last trumpet. For the trumpet will sound, the dead with be raised; imperishable and we will be changed. For the perishable must clothe itself with the imperishable and the mortal with immortality. When the perishable has been clothed with the imperishable, and the mortal with immortality, the say that is written will come true: Death has been swallowed up in victory" (1st Corinthian 15:52-54) Apostle Paul is telling us that it is a mystery the truth that when Christ returns to Earth from Heaven for His church, those believing Christians who are still living on Earth, will have their bodies immediately transformed and made imperishable and immortal.

Buried the dead is like sowing them on the ground, committing the seed to the Earth; that it may spring out of it again. When the body rises they will be out of the power of the grave and never more to be liable to corruption. At the resurrection believers' body will be made like the glorious body of our Savior and shine out of splendor resembling Christ's body. The body of believers will rise as a spiritual body. It is going to be a resurrection bodies made fit and perfect. As we have our natural Earthly body from the first Adam, same way we will have our spiritual body from the second Adam who is a live giving spirit. The bodies of the believers, when they shall rise again, will be greatly changed from what they are formally. They are now corruptible they will be change to incorruptible, glorious, and spiritual bodies, fitted to celestial world.

All the believing Christians will not die, but they will be change. All the believing Christians will glory over death as a vanquished enemy. Believers obtained victory over death through Jesus Christ. Believers must rejoice beforehand, in the hope of this victory; and when they arise gloriously from the grave, they will bodily triumph over death. The difference between a natural body and a spiritual body is that the natural body is made for life here on Earth; whereas, the spiritual body is made to life in Heaven. This natural body is under soul control, where the spiritual body is under the spirit control. A spiritual body is the one that will truly serve the Lord forever.

In resurrection we will receive spiritual bodies. As we have borne the characteristic of the first Adam in our natural birth, same way we shall bear the image of Jesus Christ in our resurrection bodies. Our present body is not made for the kingdom of God, it cannot live eternally with God in a natural body, our present bodies are subject to disease, decay and decomposition, and it will not be good for life in Heaven. When the dead in Jesus Christ are raised and those who are still alive are changed with them therefore, through faith in Jesus Christ we have victory over death and the grave forever.

"Now if I drive out demons by Beelzebub, by whom do your followers drive them out? So the, they will be your judges. But if I drive out demons by the finger of God, then the kingdom of God has come to you" (Luke 11:19-20) The Lord Jesus Christ taught the people during His Earthly ministry that the success of God's kingdom on Earth is in direct proportion to the destruction of the devil's work and the deliverance of sinners from the bondage to sin and the demonic, because Satan will resist the coming of Jesus Christ's kingdom on Earth.

Chapter 12

Christ the Consummation of Peace in Wisdom

Christ is the consummation of peace in wisdom the Scripture revealed: "For since in the wisdom of God the world through its wisdom did not know Him, God was pleased through the foolishness of what was preached to save those who believe. Jews demand miraculous signs and Greeks look for wisdom, but we preach Christ crucified; a stumbling block to Jews and foolishness to Gentiles, but the those whom God, has called, both Jews and Greeks, Christ, the power of God and the wisdom of God. For the foolishness of God is wiser than man's wisdom, and the weakness of God is stronger than man's strength" (1st Corinthians 1:21-25). Jesus Christ is the consummation of peace in wisdom because the wisdom of this world is a wisdom that excludes God. The world's wisdom emphasizes people to self-sufficiency; they make people or themselves the highest authority and they refuse to acknowledge the revelation of God in Jesus Christ.

Therefore, human being's wisdom is foolishness because through it people of this world have failed to find the truth, or have failed to come to know their Creator. Believing Christians worldview when derived from the Word of God and from the revelation of the Cross will be fundamentally incompatible with the worldview of people's wisdom. The preaching of the Gospel and the message of the Cross must never be compared to Philosophy, Science, or any other human wisdom. People of this world did not know the wisdom of God; they don't know God had to offer His Son for the sin of the people in the world. They refuse to comprehend the message of the lordship of the crucified Lord and the resurrection of Jesus Christ.

They must realized that God's foolishness and weakness in Christ Jesus' crucifixion provided a solution for the sin problem of the people of this world that has confused and defeated all the world wisdom and power in world history. Therefore, God's weakness is stronger than people of this world greatest strength. Apostle Paul emphasizes in this two verses that God's standards and values are different from those accepted by the people of the world. A day is coming when God will overthrow the process of all worlds' false standard and wisdom. The power and the wisdom of God through Jesus Christ and the Cross will continue to produce a spiritual salvation in people of this world in the ages to come that will nullify the esteemed things of this present age.

Through Jesus Christ crucifixion and His resurrection, as well as through choosing the lowly things of this world, God will nullify the esteemed things of this present age. God will put an end into all the people's Philosophical theories. And Psychological theories and all other worldly systems. The people of this world will know and see clearly truth that it is through Jesus Christ, in Jesus Christ, and with Jesus Christ; the believers' receive the wisdom from God and as well experience righteousness, sanctification and redemption as long as they have given their lives to Jesus, and are joined with Jesus Christ.

Christ Jesus is the source of all blessings; all the believing Christians must concentrate on the central truth of the Gospel, which is the redemption through Jesus and on the power of the Holy Spirit, know their limitations, their inadequacy, their inner fear and trembling. They must rely not on themselves, but on Jesus Christ's message and on the Holy Spirit, which will result in a great measure with greater demonstration of the power of the Holy Spirit in their lives. The message of the Cross did not only involve wisdom and truth, but it involved the activities and active power of God coming down from Heaven as a human being in order to save, lead, drive out demons and redeem people of this world from their sins and from the power of sin.

All those who are saved Jesus Christ is the wisdom of God and the power of God. They were enlightened by the Holy Spirit they discern more glorious discoveries of God's wisdom and power of crucifixion of Jesus Christ by believers through the Holy Spirit's revelation and the illumination. All believers must read the Scriptures daily, so that the Holy Spirit might illuminates their understanding of the truth, that the Holy Spirit might also give faithful believers a strong assurance of the divine Word of God through the Scripture. The Holy Spirit will be able to expound the Word of the Gospel to the people's heart as they witness and preach to them that the Holy Spirit makes the word of the Scripture bear more and more fruits.

All Christian believers that listened to the preaching and teaching of the Gospel, they are the ones that discover true wisdom. It is not a worldly wisdom, but it is a divine wisdom from the Spirit of God, which no one can reveal, but God Himself who ordained this wisdom has determined before the foundation of the world to reveal this wisdom to His people who love Him. The wisdom of God taught by the Gospel prepares for the believer's everlasting glory and happiness in the world to come. It was a great privilege for all the believers to have this glorious wisdom discovered for them; what honor does Christ Jesus put on all those who believe in Him. Glory and honor and praise to the one who is seated at the right hand of God; who is the wisdom of God and the power of God to those who loved Him.

Christ is the consummation of peace in the wisdom of God: "And to make plain to everyone the administration of this mystery, which for ages past was kept hidden in God, who created all things. It is intent was that now, through the church; the manifold wisdom of God should be made known to the rulers and authorities in the heavenly realms, according to His eternal purpose, which He accomplished in Christ Jesus our Lord. In Him and through faith in Him we may approach God with freedom and confidence" (Ephesians 3:9-12) the mystery of Jesus Christ hidden for ages in God the Father; God now made known by revelation through the Holy Spirit to the apostles, ministers, prophets. This mystery of Jesus Christ is God's purpose and desire to bring all this in Heaven and on Earth together under one head, and to include people of all nations in the promise of life and salvation.

Jews, gentiles all people from all nations, God created in Jesus Christ new people for Himself. Grace of God was freely given to those who believes so that they can be able to accomplish God's will; an energizing strength that flows from the risen Lord and operates through the indwelling of the Holy Spirit. God's great wisdom has been demonstrated through the church. There is a mighty treasure of mercy, grace, and love, laid up in Jesus Christ, that both for Jesus and gentiles. These blessings are unsearchable riches, which believers cannot find, it is the responsibility of all the believing Christians to preach these unsearchable riches of Christ to the people of this world.

God designed and planned that all the people of the Earth might be save with great variety, God wisely dispenses things, in many ways He takes in the ordering of His church to preach the Gospel to the gentile world. All believers have this liberty to open their minds free to God, as to a Father in Heaven. Believers must come with humble, boldness to hear from God the Father, they must expect to hear good word from Him and He will comfort them because He is the God of all comfort. The Scripture also revealed the wisdom of Christ: "Jesus Christ is the same yesterday, and today, and forever."(Hebrews 13:8) The truth is that Jesus Christ change not; this assurance provides great strength to all the believing Christians' faith. It proves that believers must rejoice and be content until they are in fullness of experiencing the gift of grace, salvation, communion with God the Father Baptism of the Holy Spirit as well as the power of the kingdom that believers will experienced in their service to God through Jesus Christ.

Jesus Christ has never change, He will never change, and He has never failed His people He will never fail. Jesus Christ is the Father's wisdom and power; He always cares for those who belong to Him from this Earth to Heaven. Believers must follow the footstep of Jesus Christ the head of the church, as He is always the same yesterday, today, and forever. Believers should be steadfast be immovable in the services and work of the God following Jesus Christ. Believers must love as the Lord loves and be one in Him as He and the Father are one.

"In the year that King Uzziah died, I saw the Lord seated on a throne, high and exalted, and the train of His robe filled the temple. Above Him were seraphims, each with six wings; With two wings they covered their faces, with two they covered their feet, and with two they were flying. And they were calling to one another; Holy, holy, holy is the Lord Almighty; the whole Earth is full of His glory" (Isaiah 6:1-3). Prophet Isaiah received a vision of God, He was cleansed and He was given a specific commission to proclaim the Word of the Lord to a spiritually blind, deaf, and insensitive people.

Chapter 13

Christ the Consummation of Peace
in Intercessory Prayer

Jesus Christ is the believer's consummation of peace in intercessory prayer. He said: "If you remain in me and my words remain in you, ask whatever you wish, and it will be given you. This is my Father's glory, that you bear much fruits, showing yourselves to by my disciples" (John 5:7-8. Jesus Christ is our great intercessor in Heaven; He is the one at the Father's right hand, and He is the one that pleads our case to the Father. He is the one that listens to our prayers and answers our prayers if He knows that what we ask for in prayer is good for us. He is the one who knows the right time for what we needed and what we ask for in prayer. The secret of answered prayer is that believers must remain in Jesus Christ. The more intimate believer's life is in Christ is through our prayer, fasting, worship, meditation on and study of the Word of God, the more our prayers will be in line with the nature and the Word of Jesus Christ; and the more effectual our prayers will be.

Jesus Christ calls believers to a life of holy intimacy and personal devotion to Him. This is possible through God's love for us, which He has poured into our hearts by the Holy Spirit. God the Father Almighty demonstrated His great love through Jesus Christ His only begotten Son, who died for us while we were still sinners. Believers must remain in Jesus Christ's love by pursuing and seeking spiritual intimacy and communion with Him. To include obeying His commandments just as He obeys His Father's commandment. Jesus Christ is our great intercessor on Earth. He prayed to the Father on our behalf before His crucifixion. "Sanctify them by the truth; your word is truth. I have revealed you to those whom you gave me out of the world. They were yours; you gave them to me and they have obeyed your word" (John 17:17, 6). Jesus Christ prayed for believers' protection, joy, sanctification, love and unity applies only to a particular people, to those who belong to God, to believers in Jesus Christ and those who are separated from the world in obeying the teaching, the word of Christ and accepted His teaching.

Before Jesus Christ's great intercessory prayers before His ascension He called on the Father to sanctify all those who believe in Him, who have faith in Him, who gave their life to Him for His Father to sanctify them. The word "sanctifies" means to make them holy, to set them apart. The evening before Christ's crucifixion, Jesus prays that His disciples will be holy people, separated from the world of sin and death for the purpose of worshiping and serving the Father. Christ prayed that they must be set apart in order to be near to God, to live for Him and to be like Him, to maintain Christ like character and to be in His image. The sanctification that Jesus was praying to accomplish is by the believer's devotion to the truth, which was revealed to them by the Spirit of truth. The truth is both the living Word of God and the revelation of God's written Word. While Jesus was on Earth He sanctifies Himself by setting Himself apart so that He can be able to do the will of God the Father; which was to die on the Cross.

Our Lord Jesus Christ suffered on the Cross in order that His people might be separated from the world and set themselves apart for God. Our Lord Jesus Christ prays for all the believing Christians, His followers and His disciples and those who will believe in Him through their witnessing of the Gospel of God. "Father, the time has come. Glorify your Son, that your Son may glorify you. For you granted Him authority over all people that He might give eternal life to all those you have given Him" (John 17:1-2). Jesus Christ's intercessory prayer for His disciples shows the heart of our Lord's deepest longing for His followers, both then and now. It is also served as a spirit inspired example of how all the servants of the Lord, ministers, pastors, elders should pray for their people, and how Christian parents should also pray for their children.

By praying for those who are under our care, our greatest concerns should be that they may know Jesus Christ as Lord and know His word intimately that God may keep them from the world, from Satan and from false teachers. Prayers of intercessor that people may constantly possess the full joy of Jesus Christ, that they may be holy in thought, deed and in character, that they may be of one purpose and as well as in fellowship, they may also demonstrated by Jesus Christ and by the Father in a way that they may lead others to Jesus Christ, they may persevere in faith and finally be with Christ Jesus in Heaven that the love that the Father has for Jesus may abide in them, so that they will be able to love Jesus With the same fervent love that the Father does and that Jesus

Christ by His Spirit may dwell in them and with them forever.

Jesus Christ prays for all the people in the world through His prayer of intercession on that night of His crucifixion. "I pray also for those who will believe in me through their message, that all of them may be one. Father, just as you is in me and I am in you. May they, also be in us so that the world may believe that you have sent me." (John 17:20-21) Jesus intercessory prayer also consist the unity that Jesus prayed for was not organizational unity but a spiritual unity based on living in Christ, knowing and experiencing the love of the Father and the fellowship of Jesus Christ separated from the world sanctification in the truth of the Word of God, receiving and believing the truth of the Word of God. Believers must be obedient to the Word and to the commandment of God. Believers must desire to bring salvation to the sinners and the lost. If anyone of these factors is missing there will be no unity or true unity that Jesus Christ prayed for will not exist.

Jesus Christ prays for His disciples and us today that we may be one; we must continually be one in Jesus Christ. The oneness that based on believer's communion; relationship to the Father and the Son, and on having the same basic attitude towards the world, the Word and the need is to reach out for the sinners and the lost. Believers creating an artificial unity by meeting, conferences, or organizations can easily resulted in betrayal of the unity that Jesus Christ pray for; Jesus will not take half unity, not cosmetics unity meetings. Jesus pray basically for spiritual unity of heart, purpose, mind and will in the life of those who are fully devoted to Jesus Christ, the word and holiness. Jesus Christ pray a prayer after He had spoken from God to the disciples, He turned and speak to God for them. Those we preach and teach the Word of God to, we must also pray for them.

The word we preach we must pray over it for God to give the increase and it will be like a prayer after receiving the Holy Communion sacrament. Jesus Christ closed this prayer solemnly with His prayers that God should preserve the good impressions of the ordinance upon them. Jesus Christ prayer for the disciples and His followers is like a family prayer, Christ's disciples were His family, and He set good example as the master of His families, He blessed His household, He prayed for them and with them. All the believing Christians must always departed in prayers, it was a prayer that was a preface to His sacrifice, which He was about to offer on the Earth. Jesus Christ prayed then as a priest ready to offer sacrifices in the virtue of which all prayers were to be made. It was a prayer that was a specimen of His intercession, which He ever lives to make intercession, which He ever lives to make intercessor for us in Heaven. If we accepted God as our Father in Heaven we have the liberty of straight access to Him, and with great expectation from Him.

The Scripture revealed: "He saw that there was no one, He was appalled that there was no one to intervene salvation for Him, and His own righteousness sustained Him" (Isaiah 59:16) the Lord God Almighty saw the magnitude of Israelites sins and recognized that there was no intercessor to turn the tide; then He decided to stretch out His own holy arm to save His people, which ultimately happened in the coming of Jesus Christ. Now it is Jesus Christ Himself who personally intercedes for us in Heaven. "Therefore, He is able to save completely those who come to God through Him, because He always lives to intercede for them. Such a High Priest meets our need one who is holy, blameless, pure, set apart from sinners, exalted above the heavens" (Hebrews 7:25) Jesus Christ always lives to intercede for His believing saints, in Heaven in His Father's presence interceding for each and every individual of His followers according to the Father's Will.

Through Jesus Christ ministry of intercession, believers experience God's care and presence, and find mercy and grace to help in times of need; such as temptation, weakness, sin and all forms of trials. Jesus Christ's high-priestly prayer for His people as well as His desire to pour out the Holy Spirit on all those who believes Him to understand the content of Jesus Christ's intercessory ministry. Christ's great intercessory ministry helps those who came to God, so they can receive a fullness of grace and salvation. Jesus Christ's intercession as our high Priest is essential to our salvation; without the grace of God, mercy and help which is continually mediated to believers without Jesus' intercession, believers will fall away from God, and they will once again be enslaved to sin and Satan's dominion, and they will incur condemnation.

The believers' hope and security is in coming to God through Jesus Christ by faith. Jesus Christ did not remain an advocate and intercessor for those who refuse to confess and forsake their sin, and who depart from the fellowship with God. Christ intercessory ministry to save completely is only for those who come to God through Him. There is no safety and security for those who deliberately sin and those who abandon God. Jesus Christ is our only mediator and our only intercessor in Heaven;

any attempt to treat angels or dead saints as mediators and to offer prayers to the Father through them is futile, wrong and unbiblical. The Scripture revealed the instruction of worship: "I urge them, first of all, that request, prayers, intercession and thanksgiving be made for everyone - for kings and all those in authority, that we may live a peaceful, and quiet lives in all godliness and holiness" (1st Timothy 2:1-2) God wants everyone on Earth to be saved scripture revealed the aspects of God's will for humankind with regard to salvation: God's perfect will which says that He wants everyone to be saved, and His permissive Will, which acknowledges that He permits many to refuse to come to Jesus Christ to receive salvation.

Jesus Christ is the only one mediator between God and man. Believers' access to God and His throne of grace is exclusively through Jesus Christ as our mediator of a new covenant and our high Priest as we rely on His sacrificial death to cover our sins and pray in faith for strength and mercy to help us in our weaknesses. Believers must not allow any other created being to take Jesus Christ's place by praying to Him or her or any object.

"At the sound of their voices the doorposts and thresholds shook and the temple was filled with smoke. Woe to me! I cried. I am ruined! For I am a man of unclean lips, and I live among a people of unclean lips, and my eyes have seen the King, the Lord Almighty" (Isaiah 6:4-5). The Seraphims are the angelic beings of high order; they serve God Almighty around His throne, they reflected God's glory that they seemed to be on fire; they sing Holy, holy, holy to reveal to prophet Isaiah the characteristic of God's holiness.

Chapter 14

Christ the Consummation of Peace
of Spiritual Life

Jesus Christ's Second Coming will be crowned with the consummation of believers' spiritual life. In the Old Testament, the Scripture revealed: "You who bring good tidings to Zion, go up on a high mountain, You who bring good tidings to Jerusalem, lift up your voice with a shout, lift it up, do not be afraid; say to the towns of Judah, here is your God! See, the Sovereign Lord comes with power, and His arm rules for Him. See, His reward is with Him, and His recompense accompanies Him. He tends His flock, like a shepherd; He gathers the Lambs in His arms and carries them close to His heart; He gently leads those that have young. Who has measured the waters in the hollow of His hand, or with the breath of His hand marked off the heavens? Who has held the dust of the Earth in a basket, or weighed the mountains on the scales and the hills in a balance" (Isaiah 40: 9-12). Salvation, blessing and comfort are all associated with the coming of the Lord to His faithful people.

He comes with power and authority like a mighty ruler, yet His presence is like of a caring shepherd tending His sheep. The truth of the spiritual life of every believing Christian should fill their heart with faith, hope and they must be prayerfully looking, longing for the Lord's nearness and special visitation, while they are looking for the day of Christ's return and of the final redemptive work of the Lord. God Almighty is the One and only who will pick and choose the individual sheep in order to protect them and carry them close to His heart spiritually. God who is the all-powerful, who regards the nations as just dust, He still cares for everyone that belongs to Him in a very personal way.

Believers must never think that God is so majestic that He does not care, or He ignores their needs and their problems of all the believers. God in His great wisdom, majestic and in His creative power, whose truths expresses and inspire His children to put their trust in Him, the One who can deliver them and spiritually establish them in His Kingdom forever. And the Scripture revealed: "This is what the Lord says your redeemer, who formed you in the womb I am the Lord who has made all things. Who alone stretched out the heavens that spread out the Earth by myself" (Isaiah 44:24). God Almighty is the only One who created the heavens and the Earth. In His second coming He is going to make everything new spiritually, He is the giver of spiritual life. "To be put into effect when the times will have reached their fulfillment to bring all things in Heaven and on Earth together under one head, even Christ. not by works, so that no one can boast. For we are God's workmanship created in Christ Jesus to do good works, which God prepared in advance for us to do" (Ephesians 1:10, 2:9-10). No one can be saved by works, good deeds of love or any efforts to keep God's commandments. People of this Earth were saved by the grace of God.

Those who are not saved are spiritually dead, they do not have a spiritual life in them; therefore, they were in darkness and Satan's dominion, enslaved to sin and moreover, they are under God's condemnation. In order to have a spiritual life in them; they must receive the provision of God to salvation; they must repent and ask for His forgiveness of their sin. Then they are washed clean by the blood of the Lamb, then they will be made alive spiritually and they will be delivered from the power of Satan and sin. Then they will be a new creation, with a new spirit, a new heart and a new name. The will receive the Holy Spirit who will live in their heart forever and the Holy Spirit will help them to live a spiritual life as a child of God.

The Scripture says: "Therefore, God exalted Him to the highest place and gave Him the name that is above every name, that at the name of Jesus every knee should bow, in Heaven and on Earth and under the Earth, and every tongue confesses that Jesus Christ is Lord to the glory of God the Father." (Philippians 2:9-11) The name of Jesus Christ is above all names in Heaven and on Earth. His name is powerful, His name is glorious, His name is merciful, and His name is marvelous Jesus Christ our Lord. The name of Jesus Christ is above all names, no one can comprehend the power of the name of Jesus Christ the dead hear His name and wake up; those who are spiritually dead hear His name and were spiritually alive serving and rejoicing in the Lord. There is no name like the name of Jesus Christ the sick hear His name and was healed from their diseases. The deaf jump up for joy hearing the name of Jesus Christ.

His name brought food to the children who are hungry in the village of Africa. Believing Christians must mention the name of Jesus in everything they are doing, especially mention His name on their bed before they sleep. Ho! What a Savior of the people on Earth and under the Earth. The Scripture revealed that: "Then I heard every creature in Heaven and on Earth and under the Earth and on the sea, and all that is in them, singing to Him who sits on the throne and to the Lamb be praise and honor and glory and power, for ever and ever! The four living creatures said, Amen, and the elders fell down and worshiped" (Revelation 5: 13-14). Jesus Christ is the worthy Lamb of God because of His sacrificial death on the Cross that takes away the sin of the whole world. The fact that Christ Jesus was slain signifies His worthiness to be praised for His power, wealth, wisdom and strength and to be ascribed the honor, glory and praise by all in Heaven.

The next day John the Baptist saw Jesus Christ coming towards Him and said, look, the Lamb of God, who takes away the sin of the world. Jesus Christ is the Lamb provided by God the Father before the foundation of the world to be sacrificed in the place of sinners; by Christ death, He was able to provide for the removal of the guilt and power of sin and opened the way to God for all the people in the world. The Scripture revealed: "Worthy is the Lamb, who was slain, to receive power and wealth and wisdom, and strength and honor and glory and praise"

(Revelation 5:12-14). Jesus Christ alone is worthy to take the Scroll of the world future destiny from the hand of Him who sits on the throne, He is the one who can break its seal and to disclose its contents.

Jesus Christ worthiness comes not from His eternal Deity but from His great activity of His work of redemption as the Son of Man. Jesus Christ must be loved and worshiped by the people of this Earth; through all the ages to come because of His humbleness to the death on the Cross. Therefore, Jesus Christ is the consummation of peace for our spiritual life. He gave His life for us, so that those of us that live; believers and non-believers must not live for ourselves but lives for Him forever. Jesus Christ is the only and one and only the Lamb of God who was sacrificed for your sin and my sin that we may live and have life in Him, life in abundant which is eternal life, life in the spirit where we will be at the presence of God.

"The one of the Seraphims flew to me with a live coal in His hand, which He had taken with tongs from the alter. With it He touched my mouth and said, 'See, this has touched your lips; your guilt is taken away and your sin atoned for' " (Isaiah 6:6-7). Prophet Isaiah instantly realized the full view of God's holiness to His own sinfulness and His uncleanness, especially with respect to his character. He also recognized the consequences of seeing God face to face.

Chapter 15

Christ the Consummation of Peace in Time of Trials & Tribulations

Jesus Christ is with all the believing Christians in times of trial, afflictions, tribulations, rejections, oppressions, distresses, persecution because He promised that He will never leave us or forsake us, He will be with us always until the end of the age. The Scripture revealed: "For we do not have a high Priest who is unable to sympathize with our weakness but we have one who has been tempted in every way, just as we are yet was without sin. Let us then approach the throne of grace with confidence, so that we may receive mercy and find grace to help us in our time of need" (Hebrews 4:15-16). Jesus Christ is our great High Priest in Heaven. He took upon Himself the punishment for our sins, by giving His life for humanity as a sacrifice; He entered Heaven where He serves in God's presence on behalf of us who believe in Him.

Christ Jesus' ministry as our High Priest in Heaven covered different areas. Christ was both the Priest and the sacrificial Lamb of God. He offered Himself for all the people as a perfect sacrifice for sin by shedding His blood and dying in the sinner's place on the Cross. Christ's consummation of peace who knows all our trials, tribulations, persecutions; He serves as our mediator at the right hand of God. He mediates the new and better covenant in order that all who are called may receive the promise of eternal inheritance and with confidence may have a continual access to God. Jesus Christ our consummation of peace is in Heaven in the presence of God to give God's grace to those who believe in Him, by grace mediated to believers by Him, Christ regenerates believers and pour out the Holy Spirit on all the believing Christians.

Christ Jesus acts as a mediator between God and all who have broken the Law of God and are seeking forgiveness and the reconciliation. Christ Jesus our consummation of peace holds His Priesthood permanently; sympathizing with all the believing Christians' temptations, trials, as well as helping them in all their needs either physically or spiritually; Christ is always there to deliver them from all their troubles and all the troubles of this world. "Because He Himself suffered when He was tempted, He is able to help those who are being tempted" (Hebrews 2:18). When the believers are tempted to fall into, or give in to sin, or to disobey God; they should pray to Jesus Christ, who also triumphed over temptation and now, as our High Priest in Heaven promises to give us the strength to resist sin and the sin nature.

The believer's responsibility is to draw closer to Him in time of trouble; Christ is responsible and ready to give help in every life situation and in every time of need. Jesus Christ the consummation of peace will deliver us from any troubles or problems believers might be facing. Jesus said call unto me, I shall answer you. Christ Jesus as a consummation of peace lives forever to intercede continually in Heaven for all those who in faith come to God through Him. He will eventually bring the believer's salvation to the final fulfillment. "So Christ was sacrificed one to take away the sins of many people; and to bear sin, but to bring salvation to those who are waiting for Him" (Hebrews 9:28). Under the old covenant, the people of Israel watched intensely for the reappearing of their High Priest after He had gone into the sanctuary to make atonement.

Likewise believers, knowing that our high Pries has entered the heavenly sanctuary as our advocate, wait with earnest hope for His reappearing to bring salvation to its completion. Christ is able to do what no one can imagine: "Therefore He is able to save completely those who come to God through Him, because He always lives to intercede for them" (Hebrews 7:25). Therefore, Jesus Christ as our consummation of peace lives in Heaven in His Father's presence interceding for each and every one of His followers according to the Father's will. Through Jesus Christ ministry, we experience the Father's presence, and we find mercy and grace to help us in time of need in all the areas of our lives. Jesus Christ High Priestly prayer for all those who believe in Him, as well as His desire to pour out the Holy Spirit on all believers, help all the believing Christians to understand the content of Jesus Christ intercessory work.

Christ's intercession emphasizes a continuation of people coming to God to receive the fullness of the grace and salvation. Christ's intercession as our high Priest is very essential to our salvation in the time of persecution and rejection. Without the grace and mercy and the help as well as Holy Spirit's mediated to believers through Christ's intercession, believers will have fall away from God and go back to be enslaved to sin and Satan's dominion which will ends in condemnation during believers' trials and afflictions and temptations.   Believers hope and security is in coming to God through Jesus Christ by faith whenever they were going through all circumstances of Earthly troubles... Christ intercession is completely and only the resolution for those who are going through persecution and tribulation through their faith in Him. Those who deliberately sin and lose their faith and abandon God, Christ will not intercede for them in time of trouble.

Christ Jesus is our only mediator and our great intercessor in Heaven, any attempt to treat angels, or dead saints as mediator by offering prayers to the Father through them in time of persecution and trials is wrong, futile and it is not Biblical for Christians to go and worship the dead such as their dead parents just because they are going through Earthly troubles. Jesus Christ is the only one who can help believers in time of all Earthly troubles, afflictions, persecutions, call onto Him He will answer your prayers.

"Then I heard the voice of the Lord saying, 'Whom shall I send? And who will go for us?' And I said, 'Here am I. Send me!' He said, 'Go and tell this people be ever hearing, but never understanding; be ever seeing, but never perceiving. Make the heart of this people calloused; and close their eyes. Otherwise they might see with their eyes, hear with their ears, understand with their hearts, and turn and be healed" (Isaiah 6:8-10). God the Father ordered Prophet Isaiah to go and let the people know how they rejected His message and they continue sinning with repentance, instead of His preaching turning their heart to the Lord, but the people continue to turn against God. People of this world are still the same today.

Chapter 16

Christ the Consummation of Peace of Those Who Die

Beginning from the Old Testament we read in the Scripture how those who die without God suffered. The Scripture revealed that: "Saul died because He was unfaithful to the Lord; He did not keep the word of the Lord and even He consulted a medium for guidance" (1st Chronicles 10:13) Saul's rejection by God due to His unfaithfulness. Up till today those who rejected God's commands will face the consequence of disobedience. The Scripture says in the book of Isaiah the Prophet: "Let us eat and drink, you say, for tomorrow we die"(Isaiah 22:13-b) This is what happens when God's people compromise with the world and turn away from obeying God's righteous ways, He calls them to repent, confess their spiritual poverty and seek His face.

Jesus Christ wants all the churches examine their spiritual state in the light of the New Testament and its standards like prophet Isaiah, Ministers, Pastors today should call people of this world for repentance of their sins, humility, tears, prayer and fasting, rather than preaching what the people wants to hear such as riches and wealth. "For every living Soul belongs to me, the Father as well as the Son - both alike belongs to me. The Soul who sins is the one who will die, the soul will not share the guilt of the Father, nor will the father share the guilt of the Son. The righteousness of the righteous man will be credited to Him, and the wickedness of the wicked will be charged against Him. Rid yourselves of all the offences you have committed, and get a new heart and a new spirit. Why will you die, O house of Israel?" (Ezekiel 18:40, 20, 31) Prophet Ezekiel makes it clear in this Scripture that children are not affected by the sins of their parents children are not going to be punished for their father's or mother's sin. Everyone in this world will be accountable for their own sins and their own unwilling to trust in Jesus Christ their Savior and to live a righteous lives.

Apostle Paul also reinstated these words when He said: "For the wages of sin is death, but the gift of God is eternal life in Christ Jesus our Lord" (Romans 6:23).

Therefore, believers who maintain the right relationship with the Lord as well as demonstrated His or her commitment to God by His loving righteousness and justice. It is this believing individual who will eternally be in communion and in favor with the Lord. God will give the gift of grace to salvation for those who choose to forsake their sins and follow Him. No one on this Earth is forced to follow the sins of their family from generation to generation.

God's gift of salvation is to bring the entire sinner into fellowship with Himself and is never pleased when a wicked person dies without repentance and dies in sin. The Scripture revealed: "Once more Jesus said to them I am going away and you will look for me, and you will die in your sin. Where I go, you cannot come. Jesus said to her, I am the resurrection and the life. He who believes in me will live, even though he dies; and whoever lives and believes in me will never die. Do you believe this?" (John 8:21, 11:25-26). For believers who believe in Jesus Christ physical death is not a tragic end. It is instead the gateway to abundant eternal life and fellowship with God the Father, Son, and the Holy Spirit.

Believers will never die means that their resurrected body will never cease to exist; they will have new bodies, which will be immortal and incorruptible; one that cannot die or deteriorate and ones that are perfectly designed by God for the greater life to come. In a new earth, unbelievers will surely die because of their unbelief. Those who live in unbelief are forever uncorrected if they die in unbelief. Jesus Christ told them that if they believe not that He is the Messiah; they shall die in their sin. Believers of Jesus Christ must believe in the power of Jesus Christ and His sovereign power of resurrection and the life. Martha Lazarus sister believed in Jesus Christ's power she told Jesus at His prayer after her brother has been in the grave for four days that God will give anything and whatsoever Christ ask for in prayer God will give it to Him.

This is an example of unspeakable comfort for the believing Christians that Jesus Christ is the resurrection and the life. Resurrection is that a dead person like Lazarus return to life; where Christ Jesus is the designer of that return, and of that life, to those that believe in Jesus Christ, the promise of the new covenant to all those who believe in Him. Whosoever believes in Jesus Christ Jews or Gentiles shall live with Jesus forever and shall not die. Their bodies shall be raised a glorious body. The spiritual life shall never be extinguished, but it will be made perfect in eternal life. Jesus Christ is the consummation of peace to those who believes in Him they shall never die.

The Scripture says: "Very rarely will anyone die for a righteous man, though for a good man someone might possibly dare to die." (Romans 5:7) Christians experiences the love of the Father which is in the Son; God's love for the believers is in their hearts through the power of the Holy Spirit, especially in time of troubles and afflictions. The love of God the Holy Spirit will continues to flood all believers' hearts with joy.

The scripture says: "If we live, we live to the Lord; and if we die, we die to the Lord. So, whether we live or die, we belong to the Lord" (Romans 14:8) All the Christian believers have and possessed one aim and one end, not self, but the Lord. Believers must know what way they walk into Christ, and they must require what end they will walk towards. All the believing Christians are one in Him as He is one with the Father.

We must learn to deny ourselves, discipline ourselves in the service of the Lord. Immediately you gave your life to the Savior you are no longer living to yourself. This is the reason why that all the people of God are one in Him; however, no matter how they differ in their lives as Jews, Gentiles, Blacks, Whites, Africans, Euorpeans,

Americans, in all the nations, all are one in Jesus Christ. This is the foundation of true Christians. Believers did not live for themselves and they did not die to themselves. We are not on this Earth to please ourselves, we are here to live for God and please Him, by doing what is pleasing in His sight.

When believers die, they die to the Lord that they may depart and be with the Lord Jesus Christ. Jesus Christ is the gain, the focus of believers in living and in dying. Believers live to glorified Him; they die to glorify Him, and to go to be glorified with Him. Jesus Christ is the center in which all the lines of life and death do meet together, so that whether they live or die, they are the Lord's, even though some Christians are weak and others are strong, yet they are all belongs to the Lord and they are accordingly owned and accepted of Him.

This is grounded upon Jesus Christ's absolute sovereignty, the fruit and the end of His death and resurrection. Christ Jesus died and raised to life, that He might be the Lord of both the dead and the living. He is the head over all things to the church. He is the Lord of those that are living to raise them up. Christ Jesus is the Lord of the dead, as well as of the living. If they are dead, they have already given up their account, which leads to judgment because both must give an account.

"Therefore come out from them and be separate, says the Lord. Touch no unclean thing, and I will receive you. I will be a Father to you, and you will be my sons and daughters, says the Lord Almighty" (2nd Corinthians 6:17-18). All the Christian Believers must maintain an attitude of separation; they must develop hatred towards sin, unrighteousness and the corruption of all the worldly systems.

Chapter 17

Christ the Consummation of Peace to Those Who live in Faith

The faithfulness of God from the Old Testament to the New Testament gives strength and courage to all those who gave their lives faithfully truthfully to Jesus. The Scripture revealed: "I will bring them back to live in Jerusalem; they will be my people, and I will be faithful and righteous to them as their God" (Zechariah 8:8). God faithfulness for the people of Israel never fail. He brought restoration after the exile as well as promises them future restoration from all over the world where they have been kept captive. God will truly manifest in His people, and they will partake of His righteousness through Jesus Christ.

God proved His faithfulness to the people of Israel again and again in the Old Testament Scripture. God will never leave them, nor forsake the Israelites His children; and they in a way of mercy, as He has promised them and they shall never leave nor forsake Him in a way of duty, as they have promised the Lord. These promises were fulfilled in the flourishing state of the Jewish church, between their captivity and Christ's time. They were to have a further and further accomplishment if in the Gospel church, but fullest accomplishment of all will be achieved in the future state. All the Israelites will be brought back to Jerusalem from where they dispersed them God promised to save them, He renewed His covenant; this is the foundation and crown of all God's promises and it is inclusive of all their happiness.

"This will be the for consecrated priests, the Zadokites, who were faithful in serving me and did not go astray as the Levites did when the Israelites went astray"(Ezekiel 48:11). God emphasizes that those who remain faithful to His will and His righteous standards while on this Earth will be rewarded in the future kingdom. Here God was saying that the gift for the Zakokites is the privilege of their living closely to God's sanctuary. It is eternally important to strive with all our hearts in order to be able to remain faithful to God and get away with all the influences of the world of these evil generations and their deceptive systems.

The Scripture says: "Who then is the faithful and wise servant, whom the master has put in charge of the servants in His household to give them their food at the proper time?" (Matthew 24:45) Those who are faithful are those who are reliable, loyal and trust worthy. Believers can depend on God in Jesus Christ for the fulfillment of His promises, and Jesus Christ Himself wants all believers to be able to depend on all who believes in Him. - Christ demands from believers to be the faithful ones who are not only depend on Him but also faithful to Him. This parable of our Lord focused on the Pastors and Ministers concerning the good servants the qualities is that He is a ruler who rules His own household with faithfulness. They must be faithful at all times in their services of the Lord.

If they continue in their faithfulness they shall be eternally blessed in all what they do, doing, or about to do. The church of Christ is His household, or His family; standing in relation to Him as Father or as their Master. All Gospel Ministers are appointed rulers in God's house not as princes but as stewards, or other subordinates officers not as Lords but as a guardians. They are rulers by Jesus Christ, upon the power they have derived from Him. The work of the Gospel ministers is to give to Christ's household their meat, or what due to them at the right time, as stewards. They are work is to give themselves to others in the service of the Lord; not to take from others for themselves, but give to the family of God whatever the master - Jesus Christ has bought to dispense what Jesus Christ have purchased through the power of the Holy Spirit faithfully and sincerely.

Ministers must give people the sold meat of the word of Christ, which He taught when He was on Earth. When Ministers give or deliver the doctrines, the work of Christ of the church, if duly digested, will be nourishment to the sinner's Souls. Jesus Christ is the consummation of peace in believers' faithfulness. Our Lord and Savior during His Earthly ministry gave us a parable of the talents, how the master gave talents 1, 2, and 5 to His servants and according to their ability before He went on His journey. And when He returns each of His servants gave an account of the talent: "His master replied, well done, good and faithful servant! You have been faithful with a few things; I will put you in charge of many things. He told the servant with two talents the same thing, and more come and share your master's happiness" (Matthew 25:21, 23-b)

The parable of the talents illustrated to all believers and those who are faithful are reliable, those who are loyal and trustworthy in the service of the Lord; just has Jesus

Christ was faithful in the service of His Father. Believing Christians can depend on our Lord to fulfill His promises, and He wants to be able to depend on His followers and on His believing Christians as well. This parable of talents also serves as a warning to us that our place and our service in Heaven will depend on the faithfulness of our lives and services here on Earth. Talents mean our abilities, time, resources and opportunities to serve God while on Earth. These things are considered by God as a trust that we are responsible to administrate in the wisest way possible to use our life for Jesus Christ as well as our money in His service.

Jesus Christ is the consummation of peace to those who are faithful in His service. The Scripture says: "God who has called you into fellowship with His Son Jesus Christ our Lord is faithful" (1st Corinthians 1:9). Christians during the apostle era, faithfully fixed their faith on the Lord who has called them to serve Him, and who gave them the great commission. All the believing Christians must be faithful to Christ Word. Jesus Christ faithful servants acknowledge with thankfulness His message to them; it is good to remember what we have received in order to know what is expected from us, and what we can give back according to our abilities.

Believers must not look into their improvements, but they must every look at what they're doing that it is by God's favor to them. The truth is the more we do for God, the more we are indebted to Him for making us for His use, and purpose. The servants produce, an evidence of their faithfulness, what they have gained. Believer's comfort in the day of account will be based according to their achievement or success; according to the uprightness of our hearts; not according to the degree of our opportunities. Jesus Christ commended the faithful servants, those that honor God now on Earth will be honor shortly in Heaven.

Jesus Christ will give them a reward, their performances will be accepted by the Lord; Jesus Christ will call the good and faithful servants. The Lord said: "Come and share your master's happiness" The Lord is saying that the state of the blessed is a state of joy and happiness; where the believers receive the vision and the fruit of God, that yielded a perfection of holiness, and the society of the blessed accompany with the fullness of joy. This is the joy that the Lord Himself has purchased and provided for them; the joy of the redeemed; bought with the sorrow of the redeemer.

"Now we know that if the earthly tent we live in is destroyed we have a building from God, an eternal house in Heaven, not built by human hands. Meanwhile we groan, longing to be clothed with our heavenly dwelling, because when we are clothed, we will not be found naked. For while we are burdened, because we do not want to be unclothed but to be clothed with our heavenly dwelling, so that what is mortal may be swallowed up by life" (2nd Corinthians 5:1-4). This Scripture is telling us that, "If the earthly tent we live in is destroyed," Jesus Christ when He returns to the believers will not experience death; rather their body will immediately be transformed.

Chapter 18

Christ the Consummation of Peace to Those Who Hope in Him

Christ the consummation of peace of those who daily have hope in Him. They daily exercise the hope of the future; His return to Earth to set up His Kingdom – with the hope of the Kingdom of God on Earth. The Scripture revealed: "You will be for me a kingdom of priests and a holy nation. These are the words you are to speak to the Israelites" (Exodus 19:6). God the Father's purpose for the Israelites for bringing them out of slavery in Egypt is to set them apart as a kingdom of priests consecrating them for the services of God and to make them a holy nation. It is the same thing with all the believing Christians under the New Covenant of grace are called to be the kingdom of priests, a holy people, people separated from all the world's ungodly ways and walking in God's righteous way and holy.

The hope of the glory of God for the Israelites in the Old Testament is that, salvation was never based on perfection in keeping the commandments, but it was based on a covenant and faith with their relationship with God. The inherent of Israelite's relationship with God was the sacrificial system that provided forgiveness for those who transgressed the commandment but who sincerely returns in repentance and with faith in God's mercy and provision of the atonement of blood. The Old Testament covenant was never complete and was not intended to be permanent. The Law in the Old Testament serves as temporary guardian for the people of God, as well as hope for them until Messiah - Christ Jesus come.

When Christ came, the Old covenant was replaced by the New Covenant, in which God the Father disclosed fully His plan and desire of salvation through Jesus Christ His only Son. Jesus Christ is the consummation of peace for all those who hope in Him. The Scripture says: "The Lord delights in those who fear Him, who put their hope in His unfailing love" (Psalm 147:11). God the Almighty Father of all mercies will delight to honor, and to strengthen those who have hope in Him. God is pleased to own the strength of grace. The Lord accepts and He takes pleasure on those who fear Him and have strong hope in His mercy and love.

Believers' fear must save their hope from swelling into presumption, and their hope must save their fear from sinking into despair. "Why are you downcast O my Soul? Why so disturbed within me? Put your hope in God, for I will yet praise Him, my Savior and my God." (Psalm 42:5-6-a) Believers must not be discouraged. Christian believers must be confident in the Lord against any earthly troubles; they must always be energized to hope in the Lord because when the soul embraces itself it sinks; if it gets hold of the power and promise of God, it keeps the head above water to those who have strong hope in Him.

Believing Christians will experience such great change in their spirit that their heart will give praises to the Lord. They will praise God for His favor for the help of His countenance, the support they have from Him from time to time in their journey of life; and the satisfaction they receive from Him because they have great hope in the Lord. Apostle Paul says: "Not only so, but we also rejoice in our sufferings, because we know that suffering produces perseverance; perseverance, character; and character; hope, and hope does not disappoint us, because God has poured out His love into our hearts by the Holy Spirit, whom He has given us" (Romans 5:3-5). Believing Christians must greatly rejoice in their sufferings because they are redeemed for good in Christ Jesus.

The word suffering means all kinds of trials that may come to believer. God the Father poured out His love into our hearts by the power of the Holy Spirit to comfort us in our trials and bring Christ presence closer to us. Christians experience the love of God in their hearts through the Holy Spirit, especially in times of troubles, tribulations, trials and sickness. Christian's character of hope in the Lord and perseverance which produces proven character and the result in a mature hope is that hope will never disappoint believers, because believers will continue to be strong in the Lord by their hope in Him.

Believer's patience during the time of suffering helps them to experience the greatest divine consolations from God. It is through tribulation that believers make an experiment of their own sincerity to God. With believers' experience they develop hope, then they are as good as gold after all their trials, and they thereby encouraged continuing to hope in the Lord. Experience of God brings hope to believers, and it also proved believers' sincerity to God's services. Hope in the Lord will not make believers ashamed nor disappoint because it is sealed with the Holy

Spirit as a spirit of love. The sense of God's love to believers will never make them ashamed in Him, and their hope in Him, or their suffering for Him will build up their hope of the glory of Christ in the life of believers continually.

Jesus Christ is the believer's hope of glory. The Book of Romans says: "Be joyful in hope, patient in affliction, and faithful in prayers" (Romans 12:12). The Scripture affirmed continuously, and with very strong word. It implies that persistence, perseverance and persistence in prayers. Believers will recognizes their struggles when comes to prayer. Not only to keep an attitude of prayers, but also to spend a great deal of time in prayer. Believers were exhorted to be diligent and faithful in prayer since it is their one of the important access to God for a spiritual intimacy as well as the means by which God advances His kingdom. Therefore, rejoicing in hope - God is served, not only by working for Him when He calls us on a mission field, but by sitting still quietly when we are in suffering. Believers that rejoice in hope are most likely to be patient in tribulation. Prayer is combined with hope and patience; believers need both to serve the Lord faithfully and sincerely. The more patience a believer exercises under tribulations, the more hopefully they may look through their troubles; there is nothing more destructive to hope than patience. The comfort which springs from the Word of God is likewise to help believers in great hope; it is good to wait patiently for what we hope for in the Lord.

"Therefore, if anyone is in Christ, He is a new creation; the old has gone, the new has come! All this is from God, who reconciled us to Himself through Christ and gave us the ministry of reconciliation; that God was reconciling the world to Himself in Christ, not counting men's sins against them And He has committed to us the message of reconciliation. We are therefore Christ's ambassadors, as though God were making His appeal through us. We implore you on Christ's behalf: Be reconciled to God. God made Him who had no sin to be sin for us, so that in Him we might become the righteousness of God" (2nd Corinthians 5:17-20). Through the creative command of God those who believed in Jesus Christ by faith are made a new creation; they belong totally to a new earth in which the Spirit of God rules.

Chapter 19

Christ the Consummation of Peace for the Vision of the World

Jesus Christ is the consummation of peace for the vision of the world, God the Father's vision to the world according to the Scripture revealed in the Book of Hebrews is that: "May the God of peace, who through the blood of the eternal covenant brought back from the dead our Lord Jesus Christ, that great shepherd of the sheep, equip you with everything good for doing His will, and may He work in us what is pleasing to Him, through Jesus Christ to whom be glory for ever and ever. Amen" (Hebrews 13:20-21). The vision of God the Father to the world is that He has planned everything before the creation of the universe that is the reason why the Hebrews writer called God the Father the God of peace. God is the only one that found out a way for peace and reconciliation between Him and sinners. God the Father brought again from the dead our

Lord Jesus Christ with His divine power by which He was raised to life so that He will be able to do everything for us that we stand in need.

The name of Jesus is above all names; our Lord Jesus Christ, our sovereign Lord, our Savior and He is the great shepherd of the sheep. All the names of Jesus Christ were given according to the vision of God the Father. All the believing Christians and the people in the world are the flocks of Jesus Christ's pasture, and He care and concern for all the people in the world not only believers. The way and the method of the vision in which God's plan enfold is through the blood of the everlasting covenant. The blood is the sanction and seal of an everlasting covenant between God and His people. Christ consummation of peace bring the perfection of the saints in every good work is the great thing which was desire by Christians.

Christ consummation of peace is the only way God the Father used to makes His people perfect in every good work; it is by working in them, so believers can be able to do what is pleasing in His sight. The Scripture also revealed: " And God is able to make all grace abound to you, so that in all things at all times, having all that you need, you will abound in every good work. As it is written: He has scattered abroad His gifts to the poor; His righteous endures forever" (2nd Corinthians 9:8). Christian believers who gave what they can to help those who are in need will find that God's grace, vision, provides sufficiency for whatever they may need because they help other who are in need, and the more they help others, the more, they are been abound in every good work. Therefore, Christian believers have no reason to distrust the goodness of God; God is able to make His vision for the world abound by His grace that the Gospel of God will reach all the people in the world, and people of this world will give to Jesus Christ for God the Father's fulfillment of His vision.

Christ the consummation of peace is the vision of the world because the people of this world have received the Word which was given to them through Jesus Christ Himself, through the apostles and through many ministers, pastors missionaries, teachers up till this present moment, they continually receiving the Word of God as ground receives the seed, and they also receive the Word of God as the ground drinks in the rain that falls from Heaven. They have kept the Word; they have conformed to the Word and they also have kept Christ's word. They have understood the Word; they were aware of all things, Christ's offices and the power of all the gift of the Holy Spirit. All God's graces and gift of salvation is from God, which was designed by His grace, for His glory in the salvation of men.

They have been justified, sanctified, they have been sealed with the Holy Spirit. The Scripture revealed: "This is what Lord Almighty says; do not listen to what the prophets are prophesying to you; they fill you with false hopes. They speak visions from their own minds not from the mouth of the Lord" (Jeremiah 23:16) False prophets hold out of God's people a false hope and security. Those who maintain the immoral and disobedient among God's people will be condemned for their evil and they need to fear the wrath of God and His judgment; they prove themselves to be false messengers and false prophets. Our Lord Jesus Christ's teaching, the central theme is the proclamation of the Kingdom of God on Earth. Christ profoundly emphasized His reason for coming to the world is to let the people both Jew and the Gentiles to know that God is love, and He wants them to put down idols, repent of their sins and ask for forgiveness which is only in His Son Jesus Christ.

The vision of the world is that God the Father, Son and the Holy Spirit will intervene the system of this creation in the very near future that will reshape all the created being men, and women animals fishes in the Ocean and birds of the air. There will be a new order of creation a new Heaven and a new Earth where righteousness will reign. Christ is coming back to set up His kingdom and His kingdom will have no end. It will be a pure Earth; this kingdom, Christ kingdom will be a final miracle of God in Jesus Christ. Christ will be the Son of Man living among His created being.

Jesus Christ second coming is the end of the present Earth and all the things that dwell in it. The consummation of a new Heaven and a new Earth will be of peace when Christ returns. Christ is the consummation of peace to the vision of the world the scripture reveals: "Lift up your heads, O you gates; lift them up, you ancient doors that the king of glory may come in. Who is He this king of glory? The Lord Almighty He is the King of glory" (Psalm 24:9-10) The King of glory is the Lord Jesus Christ. The people of this Earth from generation to generation who seek Him faithfully as all the faithful believers must pray and praises the king of glory who comes and who is to come. Believer's prayers for God's kingdom to come on Earth anticipate Jesus Christ eternal reign and the final destruction of evil in the world.

We see also in another Scripture: "For the Lord is our judge, the Lord is our Lawgiver, the Lord is our King;

it is He who will save us" (Isaiah 33:22) Prophet Isaiah prophecy about God's future kingdom on Earth, therefore, the reigning King will be the Messiah Jesus Christ the Son of God Himself who set up the vision of the world from the Old Testament people of Israel to the New Testament and till this present moment. God the Father through Jesus Christ rules the Israelite in the Old Testament. Prophet Isaiah said: "Woe to me" when He was in the presence of the Lord He realized and found out that He was a sinner. He realized His own sinfulness and uncleanness, especially with respect to His speech. Isaiah also recognized the consequences of seeing God face to face, He was frightened. God then cleansed His mouth and His heart and made Him fit to remain in His presence as a servant and prophet of the Holy One of Israel.

All the believing Christians who approach God must have their sins forgiven and their hearts cleansed by the Holy Spirit for only God can provide the purity that He requires from His people. Christ rules over the Earth and over all the creation the Scripture revealed that Isaiah realized that He was a sinner; He have offended God if not in words but indeed. All the believing Christians have a reason to cry out to God concerning their sinful nature. We are people of unclean lips; our lips are not consecrated to

God. We are unworthy to take God's name into our lips. The impurity of our lips ought to be the grief of our souls, for by our words we shall be justified or condemned.

Believers live among those who are evil. If we do not have the indwelling of the Holy Spirit we might, or it will be very difficult to live a Christian live, but we thank God for the mediator of a New Covenant who is between man and the Holy God. One of the Seraphim immediately flew to Him, in order to purify Him. Same with Christians today; those who are struck down with the visions of God's glory shall soon be raised up again with the visions of the visits of His grace and the glory of God. This was the first time that one of the Seraphim was dismissed, for a time, from the throne to God's glory, in order to be a messenger of His grace to a good person; and He came flying to Him. We can also see this in the life of our Lord Jesus Christ during His agony "An angel from Heaven appeared to Him and strengthened Him." (Luke 22:43) The Seraphim ignite life into Isaiah, because the best way to purge the lips from the uncleanness of sin is to fire the soul with the love of God through the power of the Holy Spirit.

The guilt of Prophet Isaiah's sin was removed by the pardoning mercy of God. The corrupt disposition to sin is removed by the renewing grace of God; therefore, nothing can hinder the worship or our fellowship with God. The way of communication with God the Father Son and the Holy Spirit will be open to us forever through Christ second coming; which the people of this world are waiting for. The vision of the world by Christ consummation of peace is to live with Christ forever in His kingdom. Our Lord gave us the great commission before He ascended to Heaven; which is to proclaim the Gospel of salvation to the entire people in this world, if Christ's commandments grip our hearts, believers must respond the same way as Isaiah responded to the command of God.

Christ is the consummation of peace to the vision of the world. "For I know the plans I have for you, declares the Lord, plans to prosper you and not to harm you, plans to give you hope and a future." (Jeremiah 29:11) The plan of God is all working towards the plan that He expected at the end of the world, which will come at His time. Believing Christians must exercise patience until the fruit of righteousness is completely ripe, and then Christ shall come, He will let them see the glorious perfection of their deliverance. He that is from the beginning who finished the work of Heaven and Earth and all the starry hosts will bring to completion of the blessings of Heaven to His people on Earth.

Christ is the consummation of peace He will bless His people on this Earth; with the expectation of their faith, which shall be an answers to all their prayers. While believers are waiting for Christ consummation, we must be full of prayer and supplication; we must make all efforts to abide in Him, maintained close relationship with who is our deliverer and our consummation of the vision of the world.

"God is faithful; He will not let you be tempted beyond what you can bear. But when you are tempted, He will also provide a way out so that you can stand up under it" (1st Corinthians 10:13). The faithfulness of God gives all the believing Christians assurance that no true believer will fall into sin because of temptation.

Chapter 20

Christ the Consummation of Peace of the Victorious Church on Earth

Christ is the one and only the consummation of peace in the victorious church on Earth, because Jesus Christ gave all those who believe in Him the victory on the Cross and the resurrection Sunday when He arose from the grave. The scripture revealed: "When the perishable has been clothed with the imperishable, and the mortal with immortality, then the saying that is written will come true: "Death has been swallowed up in victory. Where, O death is your victory? Where, O death is your sting? The sting of death is sin, and the power of sin is the Law. But thanks are to God! He gives us the victory through our Lord Jesus Christ" (1st Corinthians 15:54-57) Jesus Christ our ever living Savior gave us victory over sin and death. Believing Christians have everything to glory in the Lord over death, death will be vanquished He is the enemy of God. Christ has opened the grave; He conquered death when He rose from the grave. Believers must no longer fear death. The foundation for triumph is that death had its power to hurt, people of this world were one prisoner, Christ burst the prison door opens, and we were released for ever from the bondage of sin and death.

Sin is the parent of death that gives all the hurtful power. The victory that all the believers of Jesus Christ obtain comes from Christ Himself, Christ death has taken out the sting of death, therefore, death have no power over believers. A day is coming in the history of this world when the grave shall open, the dead in Christ shall be revive, and become immortal, and put out of the reach of death for ever. Believers rejoice beforehand, in the hope of this victory; and when He arose gloriously from the grave, they will bodily triumph over death. Believers owed this to the grace of God in Jesus Christ that sins are pardoned and death is disarmed; the triumph of believers over death shall be accompanied by thanksgiving to God through our Lord Jesus Christ.

What all the believers need to do to enjoy their blessings and honor God in reverence glory to Him; this will improve our relationship with God as well as exalted His Holy name and our satisfaction in Him. Those who remain under the power of death will have no heart to thank the Lord or praise Him. The believing Christian who are the conquered, or the conquests and who triumphs, they will certainly tune their tongues to sing thankfulness, and praises to the Lord. The Scripture revealed: "No one serving as a soldier gets involved in civilian's affairs He wants to please His commanding officer. Similarly, if anyone competes as an athlete, He does not receive the victor's crown unless He competes according to the rules" (2nd Timothy 2:4-5). Ministers of the Gospel of Jesus Christ, pastors and all the believing Christians who remain stead forwards, and steadfast to the Lord Jesus Christ and the Gospel will be called to endure hardship like soldiers. They must be willing to go through difficulties and sufferings and to be able to wage spiritual warfare with wholehearted devotion to the Lord in prayer. Paul gave an example of an athletes, willing to sacrifice and live, lives of strong discipline like farmers, they must be patient in seed sowing and committed to hard work; believers must be ready to endure, remain faithful so that they can reign with Jesus Christ in Heaven.

Divine faithfulness is a comfort for those who remain loyal to Jesus forever. In doing that which is good believers, ministers pastors and all Christians, are like soldiers of Jesus Christ. The soldiers of Jesus Christ must approve themselves as good soldiers, faithful to their captains, who are Jesus. Those who approve themselves good soldiers of Jesus Christ must be able to endure hardness, must expect trial, suffering in this world, and be ready to bear any problems patiently when the trouble comes their way. Believers must not entangle themselves in the affairs of this world, if they have given themselves to Christ as a soldier; they must sit separate to this worldly power. Even though, believers are still in the world they must separate themselves from the world; while they were still here in the world.

The focus of the soldier is to please His general; therefore, the great care of a Christian should be to please His Lord Jesus Christ. In terms of spiritual warfare, believers must carry it out with rules; He must observe the laws of spiritual warfare. By doing that which is good in the sight of the Lord they must do it in a correct manner that their good may not be evil spoken. Those who do this shall receive a crown of righteousness from the Lord.

The Scripture revealed: "He gives His King great victories; He shows unfailing kindness to His anointed, to David and His descendants forever" (Psalm 18:50) we see that the life of King David is a life of victory. He looks back with thankfulness, upon the great things, which God had done for Him. When we as a believer of Jesus Christ set ourselves to praise God for one of His mercy upon us; we must be led to observe many more things which He has done and which we have been compassed about, and followed all our lives. Many things contributed to David's words of thanksgiving; His advancement of the hand of God in all what He did or has done God gave Him more than what He did not dream, He gave Him boldness and strength, God protected Him and kept Him safe, in the midst of his greatest troubles.

God had raised David to the throne, and not only delivered him and kept him alive, but He had dignified him and made him great. David therefore, looks forward, with a believing heart of hope that God will still do good things to Him. His descendants will be forever continued in the Messiah, who, He foresaw, should come from his line. He will show mercy to His anointed, to His Messiah, the anointed of the God of Isaac and Jacob and to His seed forever. The Scripture says: "We will shout for joy when you are victorious and will lift up our banners in the name of our God. May the Lord grant all your requests" (Psalm 20:5). All the believers must learn how to pray. There are prayers to God about the spiritual warfare of His people against their enemies. Prayer before the battle and after the battle there should be a prayer for praises same thing with believers of Jesus Christ we must pray about spiritual warfare that we are struggling against unseen, yet very real, against forces of evil, and we must be able to rejoice for the divine deliverance from Satan and all other power of evil.

"O Lord, the King rejoices, in your strength. Through the victories you gave, His glory is great: you have bestowed on Him splendor and majesty" (Psalm 21: 1, 5). This scripture is one of the most quoted words in the New Testament because it so precisely portrays Jesus Christ's suffering on the Cross. It is a cry of anguish and grief from a godly sufferer who has not yet been delivered from trials and suffering. All suffering believers can easily identify themselves with the word of this prayer. The word expresses an experience far beyond any ordinary human experience. It inspired by the Holy Spirit, both of these Scripture predicts the suffering of Jesus Christ in His crucifixion and His victory over death, subsequent vindication after three days when He rose from the grave. David stated that His joy was in God's strength and in His salvation, and not in the strength or success of His enemies.

He also directs His subjects to rejoice and to give God the glory for the victories won. All the believing Christians must rejoice when God's blessings were given in a preventing way which makes it come sooner and prove richer than anyone could imagine, when Christ blessings come to us before we even prayed for them, or ready for them, then we may truly said that God has get a crown of pure gold upon His head and kept it there; when His enemies attempted to throw it away. God had given Jesus Christ the satisfaction of being the channels of all blessings to human kind. Therefore, the Church of Jesus Christ will be continuously victorious in the Lord Jesus Christ because Christ is the consummation of the victory of His Church.

Jesus Christ took to Him flesh; He became a mortal man. Jesus Christ in the days of His flesh subjected Himself to death; He was tempted, bleeding dying Jesus. God the Father was able to save Him from death, God the Father shows His kindness to the humanity that He did not let that suffer cup pass away from His Son Jesus Christ; otherwise, there would have been no forgiveness of our sins. Jesus Christ in the day of His flesh, offered prayers and supplications to the Father. There are many, many instances we read in the Scripture where Jesus Christ was praying. He prays in His agony and His prayer before His agony. The prayers and supplications that Jesus offered up were joined with strong cries and tears, He set for us examples. How many dry prayers, how few wet ones, do we offer to God.

Jesus Christ was heard in that He feared. His prayer was answered. He received support in His agonies; God sent an angel to comfort Him, and the Father Himself was with Him. He was able to go through death, and He was delivered from His agonies by a glorious resurrection. He had gone through death; and there is no real deliverance from death, but He was able to go through it voluntarily. We may have many recoveries from sickness, but we have never been saved from death until we are carried well through it by the power of the Holy Spirit, or until we have gone through it with the indwelling of the Holy Spirit.

Therefore, the Church of Jesus Christ continues to be great and successful because of the agonies of death and the resurrection of our Lord; believers must be grateful for what Jesus Christ went through in order to save His Church and make them glorious in Him. Jesus Christ is the consummation and the very reasons why His church on Earth is victorious and will continue to be victorious.

"The man without the Spirit does not accept the things that come from the Spirit of God, for they are foolishness to Him, and He cannot understand them, because they are spiritually discerned. The spiritual man makes judgments about all things, but He Himself is not subject to any man's judgment" (1st Corinthians 2:14-15). The Scripture is teaching us that there are two classes of people in this world; the natural also called unspiritual men, or women who do not want to know anything about God. The spiritual men and women who were been regenerated; one who has the Holy Spirit; they are the spiritually minded people and they lives under the Spirit of God's control.

Chapter 21

Christ the Consummation of Peace for Sinners and the Lost

Jesus Christ is the consummation of peace of the sinners and the lost from the Old Testament to the New Testament. The Scripture revealed: "I will sprinkle clear water on you, and will be clean; I will cleanse you from all your impurities and from all your idols. I will give you a new heart and put a new spirit in you; I will remove from you your heart of stone and give a heart of flesh. And I will put my Spirit in you and move you to follow my decrees and be careful to keep my laws" (Ezekiel 36:25-27). God the Father Almighty promises to restore the children of Israel not only physically, but also spiritually; this restoration involves given them a new heart that is as tender as flesh so that they will be able to respond to God's Words. Also, God will put His Holy Spirit in them. This work of God encompasses the new covenant established by Jesus Christ.

The Scripture revealed: "Come now, let us reason together, says the Lord. Tough your sins are like scarlet, they shall be as white as snow though they are red as crimson, they shall be like wool"(Isaiah 1: 18). God did not want to condemn and destroy His people. He offered a full forgiveness and pardon if they will repent, and put away evil, and strive to do what is right and as well as obey His word. All what a sinner needs to do is to confess their sins accept the cleansing of God through the blood of Jesus Christ. Jesus said: "Come to me, all you who are weary and burdened, and I will give you rest take my yoke upon you and learn from me, for I am gentle and humble in heart, and you will find rest for your souls. For my yoke is easy and my burden is light (Matthew 11:28-30). Jesus is the consummation of peace for sinners and the lost; He called them to take His yoke upon themselves and learn from Him. He is gentle like a dove and ready to wash them clean; He is humble in heart, and said they will find rest for their souls. What a gracious invitation from the God of Heaven and Earth. Jesus Christ graciously gives an invitation to all the people in this world to come to Him.

Those who are going through troubles of life and sins of their own by coming to Jesus Christ, obeying His directions, they will be free from insurmountable burdens, and have rest and peace by the power of the Holy Spirit. The Holy Spirit will lead them through life trials; tribulations, troubles and their problems will be gone with the help of the Holy Spirit. The grace of God will abound in all the areas of their lives. Their sins will be cleansed with the precious blood of the Lamb.

Apart from the indwelling of the Holy Spirit, it is very difficult, it is impossible for ordinary person to have true life, follow God's way, and it is very essential that all believers remain open to the voice and to the guidance of the Holy Spirit. God promised to cleanse the people of Israel from the pollution of sin, the sprinkling clean water upon them signifies both the blood of Jesus Christ sprinkled upon the conscience to purify and to take away their guilt, so that the grace of the Spirit sprinkled on the whole soul to purify it from all the corruption of the world. God promised a new heart, which will be soft, and tender, a heart that has spiritual senses exercised, a heart that will comply with everything, as well as with the will of God. A heart that was different from what they had before, a heart that will love the Lord and willingly be ready to do God's work and do what is pleasing in His sight, a heart that will stay away from the world, and most important a heart that will hate sin and sin nature a heart that will not do no evil; a pure heart.

Christ is the consummation of peace to sinner and the lost because when He came to the world His main goal was to seek the sinner and the lost. The Scripture revealed: "Jesus said to Him, 'Today salvation has come to this house, because this man, too, is a son of Abraham. For the Son of man, come to seek and save what was lost.' " (Luke 19:9-10). The mission and the reason why Christ Jesus came to this world is to save the sinner and the lost. Therefore, when the Pharisees and the Sadducees were complaining that Jesus Christ visited Zacchaeus' house, Jesus Christ told them that He came to the world to save the sinners and the lost. Jesus Christ's earthly mission is to save the sinners and the lost sheep of Israel. In the Book of Matthew Jesus said: "But He who stands firm to the end will be saved. And this Gospel of the kingdom will be preached in the whole world as a testimony to all nations, and then the end will come" (Matthew 24:14). The Gospel of the kingdom must be preached in the power and in the righteousness of the Holy Spirit and will also be accompany by the signs of the Gospel.

A believing Christian's task is to faithfully and continually be teaching, preaching the Gospel to all the people in all the nations of this world. Jesus Christ came from Heaven to Earth to seek and to save the people of this world from their sins because people are perishing without God. Christ came to the world to pardon and save as well as show us that God is love. Scripture says: "From one man He made every nation of men, that they should inhabit the whole Earth; and He determined the times set for them and the exact places where they should live" (Acts 17:26). Jesus Christ is the consummation of peace to the sinners and the lost is therefore, the Lord of Heaven and Earth. He created all things without doubt He has the disposing of all things; He is the creator of all the people on Earth, by making one blood of all the people in all the nations.

Jesus Christ is the founder and disposer; He disposed people into communities. He made them all of one blood, of one and the same nature, that hereby they might engage in mutual affections and assistance, as fellow creatures as brothers and sisters. The Scripture revealed: "This is good, and pleases God our Savior, who wants all men to be saved and to come to knowledge of the truth.

For there is one God and one mediator between God and men, the man Christ Jesus, who gave Himself as a ransom for all men the testimony given in its proper time." (1st Timothy 2:3-6) This Scripture reveals two aspect of God's Will for the people of the world in regards to salvation. God's perfect will, which says that He wants everyone to be saved, as well as His permissive will, which acknowledges that He permits many to refuse to come to Christ to receive salvation.

Believer's access to God and His throne of grace is exclusively through Jesus Christ as the one and only mediator, as we rely on His sacrificial death to cover our sins. Jesus Christ is the mediator He wants all men to be saved and come to the knowledge of the truth - people are more concern to get the knowledge of the truth because it is the way to be saved and mediation gave Himself a ransom for all people. He does not want anyone to perish, He wants them to come to the knowledge of the truth and be saved. As God's mercy extend itself to all His works, so the mediation of Jesus Christ extends to all the people of the Earth; so that no one will be under the law which is the covenant of works, but they will be under the grace which is a covenant of God. Christ dies for the sinners and the lost in other to make peace between God and man.

Christ is the consummation of peace to the sinners and the lost He wants all the believers to come to the knowledge of the truth, all the servants of God, ministers, pastors must preach the true Gospel, which is the basis of the salvation. Without the knowledge of repentance no one will be saved Christ is our mediator He wants every sinners to be saved and the lost to come home to the Father.

The Scripture says: "Remember this: whoever turns a sinner from the error of His way will save Him from death and cover over a multitude of sins" (James 5:20). The believing Christians must do everything possible, make all efforts to turn back to God the lost who stray away from the brothers. Believers must be concern about the salvation of a wandering sisters and brother who because of some affliction or trouble turn away from God. If the backslider returns to Jesus Christ, the person that witness to the lost saved Him from death - spiritual death and eternal separation from God. Believers should pray that the grace of God and the Holy Spirit will convert and change the sinners and the lost. Believers are instrumental in the conversion life of the sinners; if the sinners hear the Gospel witness to them and saved separate from the world, sin and death. Therefore, all the believing Christians must make every effort to witness to the sinners and the lost in order to win souls for Christ.

Believers should follow the footstep of our Lord Jesus Christ who came to the world to seek and save that which was lost. So that everyone on this Earth must hear the Gospel preach to them in their own language and be save into His holy hands. Jesus Christ is the one and only the consummation of peace for sinners and the lost believe in Him you have life everlasting and eternal inheritance, the gift of grace and salvation. Christ is waiting for you, when He knock the door of your heart open it for Him. He wants you to be alive in Him, He is waiting to bless you with a new heart, a new spirit and a new mind; He is the Savior of all the people in the world.

"The law was added so that the trespass might increase. But where sin increased, grace increased all the more, so that, just as sin reigned in death, so also grace might reign through righteousness to bring eternal life through Jesus Christ our Lord" (Romans 5:20-21). Faith in Jesus Christ our Lord and Savior is God's requirement for receiving His free gift of salvation of grace.

Chapter 22

Christ the Consummation of Peace of the Meek, Lowly, and Lonely

The Scripture says: "Turn to me and be gracious to me, for I am lonely and afflicted" (Psalm 25:16). In time of loneliness all the believing Christians must call on to the Lord for strength and deliverance from the oppression and from the bondage of loneliness, including the afflictions that may take the advantage of their loneliness. "Though my father and mother forsake me, the Lord will receive me" (Psalm 27:10). We see here that if our earthly father and mother forsake us, if they do not care about where we are, what we eat, if we have a job or not, where we live or if we are in the homeless shelter, we must trust God who is our heavenly Father to take care of us and solve our problems. Believers must try their best, make every effort to pray and seek His face for the problems of loneliness. Those believers, who strive to dwell in God's presence during the time of afflictions and loneliness, are given the firm assurance that no matter what type of trials comes their way Jesus Christ the everlasting Lord consummation of peace has the power in Heaven and on Earth to take care of it.

Jesus Christ our Lord and Savior will never forsake His own people. Believing Christians have no reason for despair or to worry and to fear; the goodness of God the Father though Jesus Christ His Son is always reserved for them. God the Father gave Joshua His word of assurance which He also gave to all the believers today through His Son: "No one will be able to stand up against you all the days of your life. As I was with Moses, so I will be with you; I will never leave you nor forsake you" (Joshua 1:5). All the believing Christians must be glad because no matter how we are alone in our situation in life, Jesus Christ will never live us nor forsake us. God the Father's foundation of His promise for Joshua never fails, likewise today God's commitment to all those who believe in Him and those who put their faith in Him, during their journey and conquest of faith will never fails.

God the Father's abiding presence with all the believers will be in reality through His only Son Jesus Christ. The gift of the Holy Spirit will help them to be obedient to God's Word. God's encouragement to Joshua, as He told Joshua to be rest assured that as He was always with Moses, and Moses did a great work for Him, He will likewise be with Joshua, so that He will be able to carry out God's commandments. God's word of assurance and presence will always be a great comfort to all the believers including pastors, ministers of the Word of God that the same grace which was sufficient for those in the Old Testament before them will not lack anything they need to serve the Lord. Those servants of the Lord, the missionaries, the same grace which was sufficient for those that were before them, shall be sufficient for them, for those that obey the Lord and go where He sent them. They shall have Him wherever they go and in whatever they do.

The presence of the Lord shall never be withdrawn from them. This is promise of God to Joshua is also applied to all the believers today. Believers will have victory over their enemies because of the presence of their Lord. The Scripture revealed: "David expresses His dependence He had upon God, David did not depend upon His servants, or His soldiers but He relied entirely upon God the Father as someone who has prospect to help and be secured from many creatures. Those people that put their trust and faith towards the Lord shall never be put to shame, their expectation will always be upon Him and they will never be lonely because the Lord of host will always be with them, never leave them nor forsake them. The Scripture revealed: "For you are a people holy to the Lord your God. Out of the peoples on the face of the Earth, the Lord has chosen you to be His treasure possession" (Deuteronomy 14:2). Sometimes we must think that we are lonely, but God might separate us so that He can use us for His glory. Believers must pray and seek the face of the Lord concerning their loneliness so that they can know that the Lord allows it in order to use them for the work of the Gospel.

God elected His own people before the foundation of the world to be conformed to the image of His Son. He did not chose believers because of their own dedication and subjection a peculiar people to Him above all the people in the world, but He chose them that they might be so by His grace. Christian's believers were separated and set apart for God, according to how they were devoted to His services, designed for His praise and as well as how they were governed by the Holy law of God; graced by a holy tabernacle, and the holy ordinances relating solely on His service. "For your maker is your husband the Lord Almighty is His name - the Holy One of

Israel is your redeemer; He is called the God of all the Earth" (Isaiah 54:5) The Lord God Almighty was telling His people that they should not fear, thinking that their disgrace or affliction, loneliness will continue forever. Believing Christians who are afflicted and going through loneliness will soon see the judgment of God which will give way to the salvation of God. God almighty will have mercy and compassion on His people and He will bring great restoration to their lives.

The shame of their youth will be wiped away completely. Grace of God will abound in their lives. The Lord will comfort His church and honor them; the Lord stand firmly with His church, Christ is the husband of the church as the prophet Isaiah said: "Thy maker is thy Husband," Jesus Christ is the maker of the Church by whom she is formed into His people we are part of His body, His flesh and His bones. Christ Jesus is our redeemer, by whom she is brought out of captivity, the bondage of sin, the slavery of sins, and sin nature. Christ is He that espoused her to Himself: Christ is the Lord of hosts, the Holy one of Israel who presided in the affairs of the Old Testament church people and who was the mediator of the Old Testament covenant when it was made by God through Abraham. Jesus Christ knows how to solve the problem of lonely believers on this Earth because He bought her with His precious blood. He is the consummation of peace to lonely and afflicted.

"There, since we have been justified through faith, we have peace with God through our Lord Jesus Christ, through whom we have gained access by faith into this grace in which we now stand. And we rejoice in the hope of the glory of God" (Romans 5:1-2). One of the important benefits of justification through faith is mentioned here in these Scripture, which is peace with God.

Chapter 23

Christ the Consummation of Peace of Those Who are Blessed, Happy, Meek & Holy

The Scripture revealed: "Blessed are those who mourn, for they will be comforted. Blessed are the meek for they will inherit the Earth" (Matthew 5:4-5). The sermon on the Mount solely contains the revelation of God's principles of righteousness by which Christians believers are to live through faith in the Son of God and through the indwelling power of the Holy Spirit. All those who give their life to Jesus Christ faithfully and truthfully belong to the Kingdom of God must have an intense hunger and thirst for the righteousness taught in Christ's Sermon on the Mount. Scripture revealed to us that to mourn means to grieve over our weaknesses in relation to God's standard of righteousness and in the power of His kingdom. Believers must also mourn over the things that displeasing to God and that grieves Him.

Believers must align their feelings in sympathy with the feelings of God, and to be afflicted in their spirit over the sin, the immoralities and cruelty that are manifested in the world. Those who mourn are comforted by receiving righteousness from the Father of peace, and joy in the Holy Spirit. By doing this they will in turn be very happy in the Lord. The meek are those who are humble in the spirit and they are those who are submissive before God. They are the Christian believers who find their refuge in the Lord Jesus Christ and are committed their life entirely to His lordship. Those believers are more concerned about God's services and God's people than about what might happen to them personally. Therefore, the meek, those who put the work of God first in their lives will by no means and by no doubt inherit the Earth.

The Gospel of God begins with blessings, and each blessing Jesus Christ pronounces it's in double intention. And is also shown where true happiness comes from as well as what consists as true happiness. This is to show people of this world their blindness as well as to correct their mistakes about world happiness. People intended to pursue blessedness, but most of their mistakes ended and formed a wrong notion of happiness; by this they missed the road to happiness. In a general opinion blessed are they that are rich and great, and honorable in the world; those that spend their days in mirth, and their years in pleasure; that eat the fat, and drink the drink the sweet, carry all before them with a high hand. Our Lord Jesus comes to give us quite another different notion of blessedness and the blessed people.

The beginning of Christian's work must be to take His measures of happiness from those maxims, and to direct His pursuits of happiness according to the command of Christ. Happiness is designed to remove all the worldly discouragements to the weak and the poor of those who receive the Gospel. A believer's happiness must depend on whose heart was upright with God, and how happy are they to honor God and in His privileges of His Kingdom. Happiness is designed to win souls for Jesus Christ. Seen how gracious are the work of His hands, and proclaimed the gracious words of the Gospel of God with their mouth, with love and sweetness. Happiness is designed to settle and sum up the agreement between God and man. To know the scope of the divine revelation, and to let believers know what God expects from them, and what they may then expect from God.

The way of happiness is fully set forth with God's Word and is opened, and makes way for some wiser decisions, the way of happiness and blessedness of Jesus Christ is different from the world. Christ the consummation of peace; He is the only one that has true happiness that will prevail and follow to all the believing Christians. Chris is the consummation of peace to those who are happy; Prophet Isaiah said: "But those who hope in the Lord will renew their strength. They will soar on wings like eagles; they will run and not grow weary, they will walk and not be faint" (Isaiah 40:31). A believer's hope in the Lord renews their strength and hope in the Lord is to trust the Lord fully with our lives; it involves looking to Him as our source of help and grace in our time of need. Believing Christians that hope in the Lord always receive the promise of the Lord. God will strengthen them; revive them in the middle of exhaustion and weakness of suffering and in any form of trials.

The Lord will give them the ability to rise above their difficulties like an eagle that soars into the sky; and the ability to run spiritually without tiring and to walk steadily forward without fainting when God delays. The Lord promises that if His people will patiently trust Him, He will provide whatever is needed to sustain them constantly. He is the source of our life; He is the everlasting and the Almighty God. The Lord God is the beginning and He is the end, therefore, nothing is impossible for Him to do for His people. He is the creator of things in Heaven and all the things on Earth, and therefore, He is the rightful ruler of all the souls of every human being and is able to save His Church, as He was the first born, the maker of the world. He upholds the entire creation, He faints not and He has never grows weary; He upholds the whole creation, as well as governs all the creatures He has the power to relieve His Church when they were brought low.

The Lord gives strength to His people, and also helps them to help themselves. The Lord helps the weak, and those who are distressed; He will help those who are willing for His help, those who seek Him with humble dependence upon Him, by faith rely upon the Lord. Those who commit themselves to the Lord's guidance shall find that God will never fail and He will not fail them. The Lord will bless them with sufficient grace, He shall renew their strength, they shall soar upward, upward towards the Lord, and they shall press forward, forward towards Heaven. Believers will walk with the Lord, they shall run, they will rejoice in the Lord, in the commandment of the Lord cheerfully, joyfully throughout their lives. The Scripture says: "And we know that in all things God works for the good of those who love Him, who have been called according to His purpose" (Romans 8:28). This verse of the Scripture greatly encourages all the Christian believers to be happy in the Lord no matter where they are on this Earth; and no matter what they are going through in their lives.

All God's children must endure suffering in this life. God will bring great good out of all their affliction, trials, persecution and suffering; the good that God works is conforming us to the image of Christ Jesus and it will ultimately, bring our glorification. Jesus Christ's provisions and providence for the good of all who loved Him will never fail. Those who love the Lord will make the best of all He does, and take all in good pleasure. Not according to any merit or descent of ours, but according to the Lord's gracious purposes. All the providence of God belongs to them - merciful, providence, and afflicting providence. They are for the good of all the believers, either temporarily or permanently good, as least, for their spiritual and eternal good. Directly, or indirectly every providence of God has a tendency to the spiritual good of those who love the Lord. The Lord works everything together for those who loved Him; based on the Word of God, we know the certainty of the promise of the Lord from our own experiences as well as from all the Christian believers.

"Not only so, but we also rejoice in our sufferings, because we know that suffering produces perseverance, perseverance, character; and character, hope. And hope does not disappoint us, because God has poured out His love into our hearts by the Holy Spirit, whom He has given us" (Romans 5:3-5). All the believing Christians must rejoice in their long-sufferings because they too are redeemed for their good in Jesus Christ.

Chapter 24

Christ the Consummation of Peace in God's Word

The Scripture revealed: "For the Word of God is living and active. Shaper than any double edge sword, it penetrates even to dividing soul and spirit, joints and marrow; it judges the thoughts and attitudes of the hearts" (Hebrews 4:12). All believers must be able to read the Word of God daily as a child of God. When we read the Word of God, God is communicating to us, and when we pray we are communicating to God. Prayer and our daily reading of the Word of God cannot be separated both of them go together for our divine strength and our divine help from the Lord. The reading of the Word of God daily is for our spiritual food, we cannot feed our physical body without feeding our spiritual soul, or body. We have to make ourselves fit to serve the Lord, go where He wants us to go and do what He wants us to do for His glory.

Believers must be physically and spiritually strong in the service of the Lord. Jesus Christ is the consummation of peace for those who daily studies, reading His Word listening to Him by reading His Word. Christ wills daily consummating to their lives. The Word of God is a connection between believers and their Lord. We enter into God's rest by submitting to the surgery of God's Word. God's Word is anything that God speaks. It embodies the very character of God Himself. It is living, active, piecing and discerning. It is also sharp and double-edged; it is like a razor sharp surgeon's knife: On one hand it brings healing and life to those who submit to it in faith, on the other hand, it pronounces judgment on those who disregard it. God's Word penetrates so deep, precisely and thoroughly our inner being that it discerns and defines the obscure which divided line between the spirit and the soul here means the human spirit; refers to the spiritual dimension of our being, our life in relation to God. It refers to our inner life irrespective of our spiritual experience, our life in relation to ourselves, such as our emotions, our thoughts, our desires, and our choices.

God's word awakens and strengthens His life in our spirit; it exposes our souls, searching where it conflicts with the life of God within believers. By being willingly submitted to the piercing Word of God, our hearts may be softened and changed so that we may truly enter into God's rest. The other alternative will be to harden our hearts against God's Word, those who do are condemned by it and perishes in unbelief just as the generation of Israelites in the wilderness which constantly reminds believers of the seriousness of our choices when we are responding to God and to His Word. All the Christian believer's rest in Jesus Christ on this Earth, and with Christ Jesus in Heaven. The way to this rest is prescribed as labor, diligent labor, which is the only way to rest; those who will not work now shall not rest here after. Let all the believers therefore, labor, and let them all call upon one another to this diligence in their working time, so that their rest will be assured.

The great help believers could obtain is from the Word of God, which will help them to obtain the rest. The Word of God is quick; it is very lively and very active in seizing the conscience of the sinner, cutting Him to the heart, and comforting Him, binding up the wounds of the soul. The Word of God is very powerful; it convinces powerfully, converts powerfully, and as well as comforts powerfully. The Word of God is so powerful to march down Satan's kingdom, and to set up the kingdom of Jesus

Christ on Earth. The Word of God will enter where no other sword can enter, and it will make more critical dissection by piercing the soul and its habitual prevailing danger and temper. The Word of God makes the soul that has been a long time of a proud spirit to be a humble spirit. The Word of God will make believer to be persevere in spirit, to be meek and to be obedient. The Word of God is a sword, which divides between the joints and the marrow; it can make people to undergo the sharpest operation for the mortifying of their sin.

The Word of God is discerned of the thoughts and intents of the heart which will turn the inmost cure of the sinner out in a way the he or she will see all that is in his or her heart all that is evil and turn from their evil way. The Word of God makes people and believers perfect in Jesus Christ. The daily reading, studying of the Word of God will let all the believers know who our Lord Jesus Christ is as a perfection of peace. His personhood, particularly which is the omniscience, omnipresence, and as omnipotence the all-knowing, all-powerful, all merciful gracious and with infinite love. No creatures can be concealed from Him and there are none of the motions and workings of our heads and hearts, but all are open and manifested to Him. Our omniscience Jesus Christ engages believers to persevere in faith and obedience. Jesus Christ is our High Priest in Heaven; He is a great High Priest. His greatness as our High Priest is set forth by His having passed into the heavens. Christ Jesus executed one part of His priesthood on Earth, in dying for us on the Cross; the other part He executes in Heaven, by pleading and interceding for all those who belong to Him.

The greatness of Jesus Christ is set forth by His name; Jesus is our Great Physician and our Savior. He is able to save to the uttermost all that come to God through Him. Moreover, Christ is not only a great High Priest, but also a gracious High Priest, merciful, compassionate, and sympathizing with His people means all the believers. Christ our High Priest is touched with the feeling of our infirmities, not only that He might be able to satisfy His people, but to sympathize with them. All believers must hold fast their profession of Jesus Christ our High Priest. The more believers read the daily Word of God the more peace they have, the more closer they will be to Christ who is the consummation of peace in believer's daily communication of the Word of God. "Give us today our daily bread". . . (Matthew 6:11). Prayer should contain daily requests concerns with the individual believer's daily needs and all other problems that believers are facing.

Apostle Paul said: Whatever you have learned or received or heard from me, or seen in me put it into practice, and the God of peace will be with you" (Philippians 4:9). All the Christians believers must practice the daily reading Word of God.

They must be the doer of the Word of God, not only the hearer. When we call on God from our hearts that abide in Christ and His Word, then God's peace will be flooded into our troubled souls. By the Holy Spirit; it involves a firm conviction that Jesus Christ is near and that God's love will be active in our lives for good. When we lay all our troubles, problems before God in prayer, His peace will stand guard at the door of our hearts and minds, preventing the care and heartaches of life from upsetting our lives and undermining our hope in the Lord Jesus. Reading the daily Word of God, staying focused on the words of God will give peace, knowledge and wisdom. The believers' prayer, petition and thanksgiving will returns in the time of fears and anxiety. They will once again be place under the peace of God that guards our hearts. There believers will be safe and they will rejoice in the Lord who is the Prince of Peace. The consequence of fixing our minds on the unholy things of this world is that the joy of God's nearness and peace will be lost and the believers' hearts will no longer be guarded by the Spirit of God.

All the believers must maintain a constant prayer, they must pray about any emergency about anything that could burden the soul and spirit, must be ease with their prayer, when believers are perplexed or distressed, they must seek God's direction and support in prayer. Believers must join thanksgiving with their daily prayer and supplications. They must not only supply good, but they must have receipts of mercy. Prayer is the offering up of our desires to God even though God has already knows our needs and desires, but we must communicate it to Him on daily basis with our prayer. The result of our daily prayers is that it will keep God in our hearts; it will bring us a greater good that can never be sufficiently valued or duly expressed. It will keep believers from sun when they are in troubles, or in afflictions. The Scripture revealed: "Therefore, get rid of all moral filth and the evil that is so prevalent and humbly accept the word planted in you, which can save. Do not merely listen to the word, and so deceive yourselves. Do what it says. Anyone who listens to the word but does not do what it says is like a man who looks at His face in a mirror and after looking at Himself, goes away and immediately forgets what He looks like.

But the man who looks instantly into the perfect law that gives freedom, and continue to do this, not forgetting what He has hear, but doing it He will be blessed in what He does" (James 1:21-25). Jesus Christ is the consummation of peace to those who daily study in the Word of God. The Word of God, either by preaching, or written cannot, or will not effectively take hold of people's life if they did not separate themselves from the moral filth and evil of the world by being the doer of the Word.

God's commandments to all the believing Christians are to set aside all the ungodly filth that permeates our corrupt society and seeks to influence believers and their families. The filth of ungodly sin will defile believers' souls and blight their lives. The children of God, God's holy people must not engage in any kind of impurity or obscenity. They must be aware that allowing any kind of moral filth, into their lives, or into their homes, including filthy language, obscenity through videos, television or the Internet which grieves the spirit and as well as violates God's holy standards for His people. The Word of God says: "Let no one deceive you with empty words, for because of such things God's wrath comes therefore do not be partners with them" (Ephesians 5:6-7). All the believing Christians must take righteousness and holiness seriously. A believer's house must be swept clean and must be filled with the Word of God and Jesus Christ holiness at all times. The Word was planted in the heart of believers immediately when they give their life to God through faith in Jesus Christ. Christians begin their new life in Jesus Christ by being born again through the word of truth. Believers must realize that a new life in Christ demands that they get rid of all moral filth that offends the Holy Spirit and they must be steadfast in accepting the Word of God into their hearts. The Word planted in their hearts must be part of their nature. Believers must daily communicate with God by daily reading of His Word.

"*Since we have now been justified by His blood, how much more shall we be saved from God's wrath through Him! For if, when we were God's enemies, we were reconciled to Him through the death of His son, how much more, having been reconciled, shall we be saved through His life!" (Romans5:9-10). All the believing Christians' salvation is in Jesus Christ's blood and resurrection life, whereby the believer is forgiven, and reconciled to God.*

Chapter 25

Christ the Consummation of Peace to All the People in the World

Jesus Christ is the consummation of Peace to all the people in the world; from the time that Angel Gabriel announces His conception to Virgin Mary. Jesus Christ left His Father's throne and put on our form in order to save us from the sin of Adam and Eve that spread to all human races. The sin was committed on Earth; therefore, Christ came to the world to correct and free the entire human race from the bondage of sin and corruption in order to reconcile people of God to God. Christ came to Earth to pay for our debt, and bless us with eternal life, which was the purpose and the plan of God before the foundation of the world.

Those who believe the Word of God are blessed; believing souls are blessed souls for the Word of God will never fail them. The faithfulness of God is the blessedness of the faith of the believers. Believers that have experienced the performance of God's promises should encourage other believers or new believers to hope that God will be as good as His word to them. Mary praises the Lord God Almighty because she knows that He alone is the object of our praises and He alone is the center of our joy. We honor God in everything He is doing for us or about to do for us, the more honor we give to Him, the more our souls will magnify Him and all that is within us will praise Him. Believer's spirit will rejoice in the Lord as Mary's Spirit rejoices in God her Savior.

Christ is the consummation of joy when He was born; the angel came from Heaven and announced His birth: "While they were there, the time came for the baby to be born, and she gave birth to her firstborn, a Son. She wrapped Him in cloth and placed Him in a manger, because there was no room for them in the inn" (Luke 2:6-7). Jesus Christ was born the consummation of peace to the people of the world. Jesus Christ called a Savior at His birth. As a Savior, He has come to deliver people of this world from their sins, from Satan's dominion and from the ungodly world, from fear, death and from condemnation of our transgressions - Jesus Christ is the Lord, the anointed Messiah of God and the Lord who rules over His people. Jesus Christ was born in a stable laid in a manger; Christ's birth was announced and attended with millions of choir of angels from Heaven. They announced to the poor shepherds in the field. The shepherds were wide-awake in the field; therefore, they cannot be deceived in what they saw and in what they heard, so as those that may be half asleep.

They were surprised with the appearance of the angels delivering message to them saying: "But the angel said to them, do not be afraid. I bring you good news of great joy that will be for all the people. Today in the town of David a Savior has been born to you; He is Christ the Lord." (Luke 2:10-11) The birth of the Savior was the greatest event in all the history of the world. It occurred in the most humble circumstance. Jesus Christ was the King of Kings: He was neither born nor did He live like a king in this life. All the believing Christians are kings and priests, saints, holy one, but in this life we must be as He was, humble and simply, we must live a humble life and make our life as simple as possible.

Christ is the consummation of a great joy to all the people in the world the angel came down from Heaven and proclaimed His holy name, Christ is the Savior of the world, from the first day He arrived to this world, since then Christ has been the object of a great joy to all who believe in Him, The Scripture says: "For to us a child is born, to us a Son is given, and the government will be on His shoulders. And He will be called Wonderful Counselor, mighty God, everlasting Father, Prince of Peace" (Isaiah 9:6) Christ was extraordinarily wonderful because He was conceived by the Holy Spirit; no one before Him and no one after Him born of the Holy Spirit. Jesus Christ is marvelous and awesome inspiring power of God in all creation judgment and in redemption. They foretell of the birth of the Messiah by Prophet Isaiah proved the truth of Jesus Christ.

Christ's birth will be at a definite time and place in the history of the universe according to prophet Isaiah's prophesy. He said that Christ the Messianic Son will be born in a unique and miraculous way. Prophet Isaiah mentioned four names that will characterize the Messiah's function; He will be called wonderful a supernatural wonder. He will show His character by His deeds and He will perform miracles. The Wonderful Counselor will be the incarnation of perfect wisdom and have the words of eternal life; as a counselor He will disclose the perfect plan of salvation, mighty God; Messiah whom all the fullness of the Deity exists in bodily form. Christ is the everlasting Father. He will reveal the heavenly Father, but He Himself will always act with mercy towards His people eternally as a compassionate Father who loves, protects and supplies the needs of His children.

Christ is the Prince of Peace. His rule will bring peace with God for humankind through the deliverance from sin and death. Therefore, Christ is joy indeed to all the people in the world, He is a great joy. The angel congratulates the people of this world, the message was delivered by the multitude of heavenly hosts praising God and thanking Him for what He has done. Believers must give glory to God, whose kindness endures forever, and His love designed His favor to mankind, and whose wisdom was incomparable in the work of the redemption of the world. The joy that Jesus Christ brought to the world still continues in the world up till today. Christmas celebration is the most celebrated event in the history of this world. Jesus Christ brought joy to the world when He ascended to Heaven the Scripture revealed: "It was now about the sixth hour, and darkness came over the whole land until the ninth hour, for the Sun stopped shining and the curtain of the temple was torn in two. Jesus called out with a loud voice, Father into your hands I commit my spirit. When He had said this, He breathed His last" (Luke 23:44-46). The people in Jesus' days stood for hours watching the crucifixion of the Son of God, the Savior off the universe.

This is one of the surest proofs of the depravity of the human heart is the fact that people everywhere in the world, they take pleasure in violence, in shedding of blood and in death. For instance, during the Roman Empire and the Greek Empire, the arenas where spectators cheered as people fought and killed each other where they threw human beings to the lions for food. The Scripture revealed that the on lookers who watched Jesus Christ die the horrible death on the Cross laughed and cheered. "You save others, you cannot save yourself," mocking and beating Him, blind folded Him and demanded prophecy. Who hit you? (Luke 22:63-64). We read every day how they persecuted Christians for their faith; many believers die in horrible manners such as burning them alive. In our modern society as well, millions of people including children find pleasure and entertainment in television and other media shows, events that are despicable, depict the human suffering, blood, violence and death. Jesus Christ our consummation of peace to the people of the world came to this world taught and preached the Gospel.

He died in order to change this attitude and to bring love and care to the people of this world. He wants the people to know and see the impact of sin on human life with eyes of compassion and to hear the groaning of the suffering of the humanity. All the believing Christians and the people of this world duty and responsibility is to guard themselves, their families, and children against all the influences that can desensitize them to human pain and to human tragedy. Jesus Christ consummated His spirit to the hands of His Father - Jesus voluntarily gave His life over to death, death on the Cross. In that moment, He went in the Spirit to His Father in Heaven. Jesus Christ the consummation of peace died so that the people of this world might have life, life everlasting. The Scripture revealed: "On the first day of the week, very early in the morning, the women took spices they had prepared and went to the tomb. Why do you look for the living among the dead? He is not here; He has risen! Remember how He told you, while He was till with you in Galilee: The Son of man must be delivered into the hands of sinful men, be crucified and on the third day be raised again. Then they remembered His words" (Luke 2:1, 56, 6-8). Jesus Christ is the consummation of peace to the people of the world because He fulfilled all His promises, He rose from the grave.

Jesus resurrection confirmed clearly that He is the true Son of God who came to the world to bless the people of this world with His eternal peace. The empty tomb confirmed that Jesus rose from the grave - If Jesus Christ enemies the ruler of the synagogue, the Pharisees and the Sadducees had taken Christ's body from the grave, they will surely will displayed Him to prove that He did not rose from the grave. And moreover, if the disciples had taken His body, as some people say, they would have never sacrificed their lives and their possessions for what they know that it is not true. Believing Christians will not be persecuting for the Gospel up till today. Jesus Christ risen from the dead, the empty tomb reveals that Jesus did arise and He is the true Son of God. Hallelujah - Hosanna in the highest. The existence of power of the Holy Spirit, the joy and the devotion of the early church proofs that our Lord is alive forever more amen.

Jesus Christ is the consummation of people to all the people in the world He ascended in a bodily form to Heaven and with the witness of five-hundred (520) people including the apostles and all Christ's followers. The Scripture revealed: "When He had led them out of the vicinity of Bethany, He lifted up His hands and blessed them. While He was blessing them, He left them and was taken up into Heaven. They worshiped Him and returned to Jerusalem with great joy. And they stayed continually at the temple, praising God" (Luke 24:50-53). Jesus Christ is the God of blessings; He is the channel of blessings. The Scripture says that He blessed them as He was taken to Heaven. God's blessings on the lives of His believers are very essential and will never stop. Jesus Christ's blessings to the people on that day still with us till today; His blessings continue to flow to all the people in the world as the Gospel is taught, preached, and proclaimed in everyone's language and in so many, many ways. Christ is the consummation of peace to all the people in the world.

"But now a righteousness from God, apart from law, has been made known, to which the Law and the prophets testify; this righteousness from God comes through faith in Jesus Christ to all who believe. There is no difference, for all have sinned and fall short of the glory of God, and are justified freely by His grace through the redemption that came by Christ Jesus" (Romans 3:21-24). The righteousness of God refers to God's redemptive work through Jesus Christ. This righteousness of God's revelation in the Gospel is not and will not ended until the power of God is totally consummated in salvation by our Lord Jesus Christ.

Chapter 26

Christ the Consummation of Peace for Consolation and the Kingdom of God

The Scripture revealed our Lord's teaching about the rich man and Lazarus: "The time came when the beggar died and the angles carried Him to Abraham's side. The rich man also died and was buried. But Abraham replied, son, remember that in your lifetime you received your good things, while Lazarus received bad things, but now He is comforted here and you are in agony (Luke 16:22, 25). Lazarus was poor all His life, but His heart was right with God. Lazarus' name means, "God is my help." He died, and He was immediately taken to paradise where Abraham is in Heaven. Believing Christians must follow the footsteps of Lazarus no matter what condition they may be on this Earth; God always has plans for them and He will carry out His plan. He will change their life to the better if not on this Earth could be when they get to

Heaven. He is the God of reward. He will reward all those who their hearts is in Him with a great reward.

The Scripture says: "Therefore, encourage each other with these words" (1st Thessalonians 4:18). The rapture of the believers will be one of the most important events in the world. Having the knowledge of this scriptural truth, all believers must encourage each other. On the day of rapture Christ will descend from Heaven for His church, the resurrection of the dead in Christ Jesus will happen; believers will go and meet the Lord in the air. At the same time, those believers who are living at that time will be transfigured their bodies, will be clothed with immortality. Believers will be removed from all the troubles of this world such as persecution, afflictions, tribulations and diseases, sorrows and all distresses, especially from sin and death. Jesus Christ will deliver them from all coming wrath of God they will forever live with the Lord. "I answered, 'Sir, you know.' And He said, These are they who have come out of the great tribulation; they have washed their robes and made them white in the blood of the Lamb. Therefore, they are before the throne of God and serve Him day and night in His temple; and He who sits on the throne will spread His tent over them. Never again will they hunger; never again will they thirst.

The sun will not beat upon them, or any scorching heat. For the Lamb at the center of the throne will be their shepherd; He will lead them to springs of living water. And God will wipe away every tear from their eyes" (Revelation 7:14-17).

The Great Tribulation is a time of the judgment of God at the end time during the rule of the Antichrist world that has rejected Jesus Christ, it is also the time of Satan's wrath and persecution against all those who receive Jesus Christ's Word during the tribulation. During the time of tribulation many believing Christians will suffer terribly as a result of Satan's wrath and the ungodly, which will not want to see any name, or things of God displayed around them or around their businesses. There will be a great conflict between righteousness and wickedness of men. God Almighty promised to remove any memory that might cause believers' suffering, regret or remorse. In Heaven, nothing that involves deprivation, suffering or sorrow, will not remain with believer - the Lord has promised to wipe away our tears. We will triumph over the enemy of God and the enemy of the Cross of Christ.

The Scripture says: "But if from there you seek the Lord your God, you will find Him if you look for Him with all your heart and with all your souls" (Deuteronomy 4:29).

All the people of this Earth are called to find God and know Him in His fullness; they must seek Him with passion and whole-heartedly with non-wavering devotion. Know God and experiencing His power of blessings and righteousness of His kingdom does not come easily, it can only happens only to the faithful who earnestly seeking Him and maintain desires for His nearness, the fullness of the power of His Spirit and His gift of eternal life. Believers must strongly stand firm in the Lord. "Yours, O Lord, is the greatness and the power and the glory and the majesty and the splendor; forever things in Heaven and Earth is yours, yours, O lord, is the Kingdom; you are exalted as head over all" (1st Chronicles 29:11). All the Christians believers must continue unceasing prayers to God; praises and honor that due Him worship Him in the Spirit of holiness as well as acknowledge His greatness and His power over all His creations.

Believers must be full of humility and thanksgiving for the privilege of having a part in the eternal God purposes. They must praise Him for all the reasons and motives for giving that come out of a sincere heart and a righteous life. Believers must be able to pray in away the prayer that God will direct their hearts to a steadfast faithfulness to Him and His ministries on Earth. Believers must acknowledge that everything they own on this Earth and what they have gained has come from God, they were giving by God, through Jesus Christ, it is not with their power, and it is through the power of the Holy Spirit who gives to all people with no partiality. Most importantly, all the believing Christians must delight and to be committed to enhancement of God's kingdom; which is the consummation of peace in Jesus Christ.

"I am not ashamed of the Gospel, because it is the power of God for the salvation of everyone who believes; first for the Jew, then for the gentile" (Romans 1:16). God revealed Himself as the one who always save His people and Jesus Christ is the one who leads through life to eternal fellowship with God in Heaven.

Chapter 27

Christ the Consummation of Peace on Judgment Day

Our Lord Jesus Christ spoke about the Judgment day during His teaching and preaching on Earth. He said: "But I tell you that men will have to give account on the Day of Judgment for every careless word they have spoken. For by your words you will be acquitted, and by your words you will be condemned" (Matthew 12:36). Jesus Christ told us that God takes notice of every word we speak out of our mouth, even the words that we did not even notice that are bad such as impertinent talk that is displeasing to God; it is the product of vain and trifling heart.

All believers and the people of this world will shortly give account for all these idle words; those words will prove us to see whether we are unprofitable servants, that have not improved the way of their speaking which are part of the talents we are talented and entrusted for good work. All the believing Christians will be at the judgment seat of Christ in order to account for what we have done after we gave our life to Jesus Christ. All Christians will be judged, without exception, the judgment of believers will occur when Christ returns. Believers must give account of their faithfulness and unfaithfulness to God as well as what they have done in the light of the gift of the grace of salvation.

The Scripture revealed: "Now it is required that those who have been given a trust must prove faithful. I care very little if I am judged by you or by any human court; indeed, I do not even judge myself. My conscience is clear, but that does not make me innocent. It is the Lord who judges me. Therefore, judge nothing before the appointed time; wait till the Lord comes. He will bring to light what is hidden in darkness and will expose the motives of men's hearts. At that time each will receive His praise from God" (1st Corinthians 4:2-5). God will bring to the open the secret activities of all people, exposing their true thoughts and motives, either good or bad will come to light. In other words, the inner lives of everyone on this Earth will be revealed exactly as they were; nothing will be left hidden and everyone will face the judgment of God.

The ministers and pastors must preach and teach the correct Gospel.

They should not value themselves as if they were the Christ; they are just a servant of Jesus Christ and they must follow His commandment. Any minister that wanted to please Himself in the service of the Lord will not be approved as a faithful servant of Jesus Christ. Believers are not to judge themselves because they judge harshly and rashly; He that has the right to judge is the Lord Jesus Christ. The Scripture revealed: "For we must all appear before the judgment seat of Christ, that each one may receive what is due Him for the things done while in the body, whether good or bad" (2nd Corinthians 5:10). All the believing Christians will one day give an account of what they have done after they have been saved. The Judgment seat of Christ is only for the believers in Jesus Christ. The judgment will occur when they get to Heaven or when Christ returns during the rapture for the Church.

The believer's judgment does not involve the condemnation by God the Father. God will examine, revealing in its true reality, all the believer's secret activities they have done while they were on Earth especially in the work of the ministry. Believers who did good will be rewarded believers should remember the judgment seat of Christ and strive very had to be one in Him, making every effort to serve Him better. The Scripture says: "You then, why do you judge your brother? Or why do you look down on your brother? For we will all stand before God's judgment seat" (Romans 14:10). Believers must not judge each other. They must encourage one another to Christ likeness and holiness

God's desire and purpose when He created the universe was to make human race to live on Earth forever. Adam and Eve fall into sin of disobedient and lost the plan of eternal life that God had planned for them. They brought sin and death to the entire human race; the Scripture revealed: "The Lord God took the man and put Him in the Garden of Eden to work it and take care of it. And the Lord God commanded the man. "You are free to eat from any tree in the garden, but you must not eat from the tree of the knowledge of good and evil, for when you eat of it you will surely die" (Genesis 2:15-17). Adam was the first man on Earth and was holy, free from sin, and in perfect communion with the Lord God. Adam was the apple of God's creation and He was given the responsibility of working under the direction of God in caring for all the rest of God's creations.

This working and good communication between Adam and God was lost not only to Adam and Eve, but to all human race because of Adam's rebellious attitude of disobedience. From the beginning of creation human beings have been bound with God through belief and through obedience to God's Word, which is the absolute truth over life through faith, and obedience is the main governing principle in Adam's relationship with God in the Garden of Eden. Adam was warned by His creator that He will die spiritually and be separated from God if He transgressed the will of God and by eating the fruit of the knowledge of good and evil.

Adam did not have faith and He did not belief in God's word. God's commandment was given to Adam as a moral test. It was set before Him as a conscious, deliberate choice to believe and obey, or to disbelieve and disobey God's will. When Adam believes in God's Word, he continues to live eternal life and be blessed with good relationship with God, His creator. Same way, with all believers today; if we believe in Jesus Christ and follow the Word of God, we have eternal life through Jesus Christ forever. If we disobey the commandment of God, we have no eternal life.

Our Lord Jesus Christ said in the Scripture: "Not everyone who says to me, Lord, Lord, will enter the Kingdom of Heaven, but only He who does the Will of my Father who is in Heaven" (Matthew 7:21-23). Jesus Christ our Lord emphatically taught that the main goal in carrying out the will of His heavenly Father was a condition of entering the Kingdom of Heaven; God's forgiveness comes to the people of this world through faith and repentance of sin which was made possible by the grace of God through the sacrificial death of Jesus Christ. Obedience to the Father's will demanded by Jesus Christ is an ongoing condition and it is the only condition for salvation; Jesus Christ made it clear and simple that it is a grace of God to the salvation of His Kingdom.

Jesus Christ says that many people in the Church, who will minister, preach, teach in His name, and the people that believe that they are His servants might not know them. Ministers, pastors, who are proclaiming the Gospel in the name of Jesus Christ, who performed miracles, cast out demons; they might not believe in Jesus Christ, or have any genuine saving faith in Him. It is good to know that on the judgment day there will be big blessings including those who die as well as there will be a big surprise because there is going to be condemnation on those who are false preachers, ministers, and teachers. They will go nowhere in the service of the Lord because He does not accept them, nor will He own them on the Judgment day.

Please that sees the church works, as a profession of religion will not bear out any man in the practice and in the indulgence of sin. Christ does not own them, He does not know them, and they have never given their life to Jesus Christ. But the Holy Spirit can still use the Word of God from them for the sinners to save the sinners. The Scripture says: "Therefore, just as sin entered the world through one man, and death through sin, and in this way death came to all men, because all sinned" (Romans 5:12) In the fall of Adam, sin as an active principle, or we can say that sin's power gained the entrance into the human race – sin and corruption entered into Adam's heart and life. Adam's sin was transmitted into the life stream of the people in the world, corrupting all the people then, and now.

All human beings are born into the world with an impulse towards sin and evil. Death entered the world through sin and people of this world are subjected to death. "Nevertheless, death reigned from the time of Adam to the time of Moses, even over those who did not sin by breaking a command, as did Adam, who was a pattern of the one to come." (Romans 5:14) The people of this world experienced death, not because they transgress the spoken Law of God with its death penalty as did Adam but because they were in fact sinners by actions as well as by human nature and transgressors of the Law of Conscience by God. God Almighty has set a date that He will judge the people on this Earth.

God will destroy all the elements of corruption in human society and remove the wicked people, the living will be judged according to the Scripture: "After this I looked and there before me was a great multitude that no one could count, from every nation, tribe, people and language, sanding before the throne and in front of the Lamb. They were wearing white robes and were holding palm branches in their hands. And they cried out in loud voice. Salvation belongs to our God, who sits on the throne, and to the Lamb" (Revelation 7:7-10) Apostle John described what He saw in Heaven a great multitude of people from all over the nations who come to salvation through the death and the resurrection of Jesus Christ and have faith in Him; they will live with God forever, those people were saved by the blood of the Lamb, these are the people that overcome the great tribulation, persecution by Satan and evil people of the world.

"*Grace and peace to you from God our Father and from the Lord Jesus Christ. First, I thank my God through Jesus Christ for all of you, because your faith is being reported all over the world. God, whom I serve with my whole heart in preaching the Gospel of His son, is my witness how constantly I remember you in my prayers at all times; and I pray that now at last by God's will the way may be opened for me to come to you*"(Romans 1:8-10). The Holy Spirit commences to transform believers into the likeness of Jesus Christ by a progressive work of sanctification.*

Chapter 28

Christ is the Consummation of Peace of Knowledge and Understanding

The Scripture revealed: "I keep asking that the God of our Lord Jesus Christ, the glorious Father, may give you the Spirit of wisdom and revelation, so that you may know Him better" (Ephesians 1:17). All the believing Christians must pray that our Lord and Savior, God of knowledge and understanding, may give those who believe in Him the Spirit of knowledge in understanding the Scripture more and more to the people of the world who do not know Him. We have to pray that God the Holy Spirit will work in all the believers in greater measure. Believers need the increased measure of the Holy Spirit's impartation, for more wisdom, revelation and knowledge concerning our services in the work of the Gospel more and more knowledge and understanding the Scripture is needed so that they can be able to help the sinners and the lost.

Believers need the abundant power of the Holy Spirit to serve the Lord on this Earth. In order for all the believing Christians to advance in grace, to achieve the victory over Satan and sin, and over death; Believers need more knowledge of witnessing the Gospel, preaching, teaching and analyzing, expounding the Word of God. God's Spirit and power must be present in the lives of believers. This power is an activity, manifestation and strength of the Holy Spirit working through believers. By this the believers' eye in His or her heart will be enlightened. The scripture revealed: "The spirit of the Lord will rest on Him - the spirit of wisdom and of understanding the Spirit of counsel and of power. The Spirit of knowledge and of the fear of the Lord" (Isaiah 11:2). The Messiah will be mighty anointed by the Holy Spirit in order to carry out His Father's will and to bring full salvation to the nations. In order to carry out the Father's will of the plan of salvation, Messiah must also be baptized and anointed same way as the believers. The study of the scripture must be on going till end of believer's life. Our Lord was teaching the people of His day the Scripture said, "In reply Jesus declared, 'I tell you the truth, no one can see the kingdom of God unless He is born again'" (John 3:3). Jesus Christ is telling Nicodemus that the foundational beliefs of the Gospel of God is in regeneration whereby, after a person give their life to Jesus Christ, there is a transition from old life of sin; to a new life of love for self, for others and love for God.

The born again Christians were born by the Spirit of God. It is a matter of the Spirit believer needs to study and have the knowledge of our spiritual body and our physical body. "And the peace of God, which transcends all understanding will guard your hearts and your minds in Christ Jesus" (Philippians 4:7). When we call on the Lord from our hearts that remain in Christ and His word then God's peace will flooded our trouble souls. Believers must study the Scripture and learn to be content in all the areas of their lives. The key to contentment is that believers must realize that God has given them everything they needed that will help them to remain victorious in all the areas of their life. They need to study in order to gain the ability to live triumphantly above any earthly troubles; the ability must be learned through dependence on Jesus Christ; it does not come naturally.

Christ is the consummation of peace of knowledge and understanding. "Now the Bereans were of more noble character than the Thessalonians, for they received the message with great eagerness and examined the Scripture every day to see if what Paul said was true" (Acts 17:11) We must follow the Bereans' example, examined, study the Scripture, compared Scripture to Scripture, so that we can easily know who are the false teachers, pastors, and false ministers of the Gospel. The model of Bereans Christians is very valuable to today's believers - Believers must listen to the preachers and teachers expound the Scriptures acquired knowledge, understanding by examining what the pastor was preaching it is according to the Biblical interpretation of the Word of God.

No interpretation or doctrine must be accepted passively, it must be examined carefully by personal study of the Scripture. It means to sift up and down, make a careful and exact research. Bible preaching should make Bible students out of hearers. The truth of every form of doctrine should be examined according to the Word of God. The understanding, the knowledge in this writing is based on spiritual understanding and knowledge to be clearly understood. All the Christian believers need the knowledge spiritually in other to understand the gift of salvation of God the Father through Jesus Christ.

"About noon as I came near Damascus, suddenly a bright light from Heaven flashed around me. I fell to the ground and heard a voice say to me, 'Saul! Saul! Why do you persecute me?' 'Who are you, Lord?' I asked. 'I am Jesus of Nazareth, whom you are persecuting," He replied. My companions saw the light, but they did not understand the voice of Him who was speaking to me" (Acts 22:8-9). Our Lord and Savior called Saul who was later became Paul on the Road to Damascus; to let Him know that His persecution of Christians that He has carried out and going to carry He doing it to Him. Christ let us know that whatever a believer is going through, or whatever someone was doing evil things to a believing Christians, they are doing it to Lord Jesus Christ.

Chapter 29

Christ the Consummation of Peace upon His Return to Establish New Heaven & New Earth

Jesus Christ is the consummation of peace when He returns to this world to set up a new heaven and a new earth. The Scripture revealed from the book of Isaiah the prophet: "Behold, I will create new heavens and a new Earth, the former things will not be remembered, nor will they come to mind. But be glad and rejoice forever in what I will create, for I will create Jerusalem to be a delight and its people a joy. I will rejoice over Jerusalem and take delight in my people; the sound of weeping and of crying will be heard in it no more" (Isaiah 65:17-19). Isaiah's prophecy foresees God's future kingdom on Earth. Prophet Isaiah blends the age of eternity where sin and death will be no more. The Messianic age which is the millennial kingdom that will proceed it begins with a strong adversative; there will be for sure a new heavens and a new

Earth. God Almighty has a plan for this present Jerusalem in His millennial kingdom.

All the believers of Jesus Christ must look forward to the new Heaven and a new Earth. As Christ after conversion in the Gospel and the Scripture stated that behold thing have passed away and all things have becomes new. "Therefore, if anyone is in Christ, He is a new creation; the old has gone, the new has come!" (2nd Corinthians 5:17). It will be a mighty happy change that was also described by Prophet Isaiah: "The former troubles were forgotten." But now Isaiah said that even the former world, this present world shall be forgotten and shall be moved when God the Father reconciled of the believing Christians, it will be as if He give us a new Heaven, if all His creatures are reconciled to Him it will be as if God give us a new Earth. All the people on Earth will be new people and all the people in Heaven will be new people because God reconciled them to Him and them a new creature in a new world.

They will be reconciled to all the animals, birds, and all other creatures it will change the outlook of the world and makes new. All the people shall rejoice. "As the new heavens and the new Earth that I make will endure forever before me, declares the Lord, so will your name and descendants endure, from one New Moon to another and from one Sabbath to another, all mankind will come and bow down before me; says the Lord and they will go out and look upon the dead bodies of those who rebelled against me; their worn will not die; nor will their fire be quenched, and they will be loathsome to all mankind" (Isaiah 66:22-24) At the end of the Messianic kingdom, God will create a new Heaven and a new Earth. All the believing Christians will be forever be with the Lord. While all those who rebelled against Him all against His word will spend their eternity in hell. The kingdom of Messiah shall be a new world, the old covenant has been set aside and a covenant of grace will be established, a new commandments will be given in relating to both Heaven and Earth, a new promises relating to both Heaven and Earth, a new promises relating to both. It will be an abiding change, a new world that will be always new.

The Gospel dispensation will continue to the end of time preaching, teaching proclaiming the Gospel will continue till the end of the age. Gospel will be maintained in a way that all the believers will serve Jesus Christ. "I will give them an undivided heart and put new Spirit in them; I will remove from them their heart of stone and give them a heart of flesh" (Ezekiel 11:19) Prophet Ezekiel prophesy that the people of this Earth will be empowered by the Holy Spirit so that they can live in accordance with God's will and law. God Holy Spirit with all His gifts and activities has made available today to all believing Christians who put their faith in Jesus Christ. This is the Gospel of promise, and it was made good to all who and those whom God designs it for in the heavenly Jerusalem.

All who are sanctified will have a new Spirit; and all their activities will be from the new principles of the Holy Spirit; they will walk by new rules, and aim to the ends. A new name, or a new face, will not serve without a new Spirit. This is God's work, and it is His gift by promise. Believers' practices will be conform to those principles, walk with God in His statues, in conversation, and they will keep God's ordinances in all their activities of religions worship. The Scripture revealed, "He has made us a competent as ministers of a new covenant - not of the letter but of the spirit; for the letter kills, but the spirit gives life." (2nd Corinthians 3:6) The letter kills means that it is not the laws, or a written Word of God itself that destroy. Rather, Holy Spirit demands of the law without the Holy Spirit the demands of the Law without the Holy Spirit's life and power, life will be very hard to live a Christian's life, without the Holy Spirit people are living a life that brings condemnation.

Through salvation in Jesus Christ the Holy Spirit gives to all the believers a spiritual life and power in order for them to fulfill the will of God; with the power of the Holy Spirit the letter will not be able to kill, and will no longer kills; instead it will become the source of the revelation and life. All believers are the instruments of God to the work of redemption and salvation. Whatever we are doing in our lives that is not focused on the glory of God, a believers' heart will be made softened and made new by the divine grace of God. A new and old believing Christian must live upon His spiritual presence and upon the comfort it affords. A thorough change of the heart makes people a new creature, that have a new heart and a new nature - God the Father has reconciled us to Himself through our Lord Jesus Christ, all things relating to a believers' reconciliation by Jesus Christ are of God, who by the mediation of Jesus Christ has reconciled us and the people of the world to Himself.

"Therefore, if anyone is in Christ, He is a new creation; the old has gone, the new has come! All this is from God, who reconciled us to Himself through Christ and gave us the ministry of reconciliation: that God was reconciling the world to Himself in Christ, not counting men's sins against them. And He has committed to us the message of reconciliation. We are therefore, Christ's ambassadors, as though God were making His appeal through us. We implore you on Christ's behalf: Be reconciled to God. God made Him who had no sin to be sin for us, so that in Him we might become the righteousness of God" (2nd Corinthians 5:17-21). We are a new creature through the creative command of God those who accept Jesus Christ by faith are made a new creation; they are made up of people that belong to God totally in a new world in which the spirit rules.

The believing Christians become a new person, which was renewed after God's image. Believers were renewed in knowledge and understanding; they will live a life of holiness. Reconciliation is one of the aspect works of Jesus Christ in redemption - the restoration of the sinners to a fellowship and to a good relationship with God. Through Jesus Christ atoning death, God has removed the barrier of sin and open a way for sinners to return to God. Therefore, reconciliation becomes effective for each person through personal repentance and faith in Jesus Christ. The church has been given the ministry of reconciliation, calling all the people in the world to be reconciled to

God the Scripture says: "Christ became a sinner in order to be able to take away our sins. God the Father made Jesus Christ the object of His judgment when Jesus Christ became an offering for our sins on the Cross.

In taking our punishment, Jesus Christ made it possible for God to forgive sinners. In Jesus Christ believers become the righteousness of God. It is the experiential righteousness of the children of God as a new creation who will live in the new Heaven and in the new Earth. Believing Christians become a new creation as well as fulfilling the ministry of reconciliation as a representative of God and His righteousness on this Earth. God's righteousness is manifested and experienced by all the believing Christians in the world only if they remain in Christ Jesus; live in union with Him, fellowship with Jesus Christ do we become the righteousness of God. As God is willing to be reconcile to us, believers must be willing, to make all efforts to be reconciled to God. The Scripture revealed: "At that time His voice shook the Earth, but now He has promised, once more I will shake not only the Earth but also the heavens. The words once more indicate the removing of what can be shaken that is, created things - so that what cannot be shaken may remain" (Hebrews 12:26-27). God will one day according to the

Hebrews writer bring down the present world order and shake to pieces the whole material universe; the present form of the world is not eternal it will be destroyed by fire and replaced by a new Heaven and a new Earth. The only thing that will remain and survive will be the present form will be the Kingdom of God and those who belongs to the kingdom.

Because it was the sound of the Gospel triumphed that a new kingdom was created for God in the world, which can never be shaken or be removed. This change was made for all the people in the world, and it was change once and for all. Believers cannot worship God acceptably, unless the worship Him with godly reverence and fear. As there is faith, there is also a holy fear; it is necessary for the acceptable worship. It is by the grace of God that enables believers to worship God in the right manners. Apostle Peter said: "But in keeping with His promise we are looking forward to a new Heaven and a new Earth, the home of righteousness" (2nd Peter 3:13). "For He was looking forward to the city with foundations, whose architect and builder is God" (Hebrews 11:10). Abraham knew that the Earthly land of promise was not the end of His life. It pointed beyond to the heavenly city that God had prepared for His faithful servants, Abraham serve as an example of all the people of God.

Traveling through this world on our way to God's city and His home He prepared for us in Heaven. The time when people of this world think to be the most improper and unlikely, and when therefore, they think that they are most secure, will be the time of the Lord's coming. The Scripture said: " The day of the Lord will come as a thief in the night" (2nd Peter 3:10) All believers must pass through the fire, which shall be a consuming fire to all that sin has brought into the world, though it may be but a refining fire to the works of God's hand. There is going to be a great difference between Christ first coming and His second coming to the world. Help us Lord Jesus Christ and prepare all the believing Christians to be ready for your second coming.

The Scripture revealed: "Him who over comes I will make a Pillar in the temple of my God, Never again will He leave it. I will write on Him the name of my God and the name of the city of my God, the new Jerusalem, which is coming down out of Heaven from my God; and I will also write on Him my new name. He who has an ear; let Him hear what the spirit says to the churches. Then I saw a new Heaven and a new Earth, for the first Heaven and the first Earth had passed away, I saw the Holy City, the new Jerusalem, coming down out of Heaven from God, prepared as a bride beautifully dressed for her husband" (Revelation 4:1) The final goal and the expectation of the redeemed are a new transformation and redeemed world where Jesus Christ will lives with His people and righteousness dwells in holy perfection.

In order to erase all the traces of sin in the world there must be a destruction of the present Earth; Stars and Galaxies of Stars, Heaven and Earth will be shaken, and will vanished like smokes, the stars will be dissolved and the elements will be destroyed. The new Earth will become the dwelling place of both humans and God. All the redeemed will possess bodies like Christ's resurrection body, ones that are real, visible and tangible, but incorruptible and the one that is immortal. The new Jerusalem has already exists in Heaven; it will soon come to the Earth as the city of God for which Abraham and all of God's faithful waited, and of which God is the planner and the builder. The new Earth will become God's dwelling place, and He will remain with His people forever amen.

Jesus Christ is the consummation of peace now and forever, in a new heaven and a new earth where righteousness will dwell. Blessed is Jesus Christ our Lord and Savior, and blessed are all His body, His church in Heaven and on the Earth. Through Jesus Christ, with Jesus Christ, in Jesus Christ, and in the unity of the Holy Spirit the Holy Trinity who is forever one God. Amen The Scripture revealed that Apostle Paul urged all the believing Christians to lead a life that is worthy of Christ's calling, in all the areas of their lives in which they have been called either as pastors, ministers, missionaries, medical doctors, lawyers and so on and so forth. "Be completely humble and gentle; be patient, bearing with one another in love. Make every effort to keep the unity of the Spirit through the bond of peace. There is one body and one Spirit – just as you were called to one hope when you were called – one Lord, one faith, one baptism; one God and Father of all, who is over all and through all and in all" (Ephesians 4:2-6).

This is very essential to the Christian's faith and unity the confession that there is only one Lord Jesus Christ's work of redemption which is complete, perfect and sufficient; there are no other redeemers and no other mediators that can give a believing Christian complete salvation. All the believing Christians must draw near to

God the Father, through Jesus Christ, God the Son; God was revealed in Jesus Christ.

There is no Lordship of Jesus Christ apart from the affirmation that the Lord Jesus Christ has the ultimate authority for the believer, and the authority of Christ is communicated in God the Father's written Word. "For by him all things were created things; in heaven and on earth, visible and invisible, whether thrones, or powers or rulers or authorities, all things were created by him and for him" (Colossians 1:16). In Jesus Christ all things whether material or spiritual, owed their existence to Christ Jesus' redemptive work as the agent in creation; all things are held together in Jesus Christ, and in Him they were sustained.

Also, in another Scripture: "Through him all things were made without him nothing was made that has been made. In him was life, and that life was the light of men. The light shines in the darkness, but the darkness has not understood it" (John 1:3-5). The light of Jesus Christ shines in an evil and sinful world, which is controlled by Satan and his evil workers. The majority of the people in the world have not accepted Christ's life or light; they are still in darkness. Jesus Christ illumines with the power of the Holy Spirit, all who hear the Gospel by imparting a measure of grace and understanding the order that they may freely choose to accept or reject the message of the Gospel that will make them saved or make them unsaved. Without the light of Jesus Christ, people will be in darkness. There is no other light by which people in the world may know the truth, see the truth, and be saved.

The Scripture concluded that: "For from him and through him and to him are all things. To him be the glory forever! Amen" (Romans 11:36). The power of God profoundly expresses the awesome power of God that to humans is incomprehensible wisdom, and the judgment of God is also unattainable in the redemptive history. The depth of the knowledge of God is also incomprehensible – we just have to say in a loud voice: "To him be the glory forever! Amen"

"What shall I do, Lord? I asked. Get up, the Lord said, and go into Damascus. There you will be told all that you have been assigned to do. My companions led me by the hand into Damascus, because the brilliance of the light had blinded me" (Acts 22:10-11). Jesus Christ demonstrated His power of all knowing, all-powerful and all merciful and mighty God, as well as His power of forgiveness of our sins. Most importantly, He gave the blessed assurance that He is at the right hand of the Father and He sees everything and know everything, Christ is alive forever! Hallelujah.

Chapter 30

Christ the Consummation of Peace Forevermore

The return of Jesus Christ is the consummation of spiritual life of all those who gave their life to Him - all the believing Christians in the whole Earth. The return of Jesus Christ will be the consummation of all things and the goal of Jesus Christ in coming to the world according to the Word of God beginning from the Old Testament. The Scripture revealed: "And that you may love the Lord your God, listen to His voice, and hold fast to Him. For the Lord is your life, and He will give you many years in the land He swore to give to your fathers, Abraham, Isaac and Jacob" (Deuteronomy 30:20). In the New Testament His word of promise of God applies to all who sincerely receive Jesus Christ as their Lord and Savior. Believers were assured that if they love God above all else and neither depends on Him, instead of worldly materials security, the Lord will never deserted nor forsake them. He will be their helper and comforter through the power of the Holy Spirit; because of this promise, believer must be strong and they must be courageous, persevere through trials, they will resists temptations, they will trust in the Lord and they will be fully obey is commandment.

The children of Israel were commanded to maintain their relationship with God by loving Him and by listening to His voice. In order to express that obedience, however, they must recognize their inability to fulfill the law and they must bring sacrifices of atonement for their shortcoming. Life and salvation were never promised as a reward for perfect obedience; the law assumed the imperfection of faith and obedience on the part of God's people and therefore, it provided the sacrificial system that atoned for sin. Therefore, children of Israel's ultimate hope rested in God the Father's mercy and grace. Jesus Christ is the consummation of peace forever: "For from Him and through Him and to Him are all things to Him be glory forever!"(Romans 11:36) Apostle Paul expresses the depth of God's knowledge in his life. The awesomeness of God the Father and the profound and humanly incomprehensible wisdom and judgments of God, in redemptive history related to Israel what else we can say then to praise God, who all the glory belongs. Jesus Christ put on our human flesh; He became the visible of the invisible God. He said to Phillip: "Don't you know me, Philip, even after I have been among you such a long time? Anyone who has seen me has seen the Father. How can you say, show us the Father? Don't you believe that I am in the Father, and that the Father is in me? The words I say to you are not just my own. Rather, it is the Father, living in me, who is doing His work. Believe me when I say that I am in the Father and the Father is in me; or at least believe on the evidence of the miracles themselves" (John 14:9-11). All the believing Christians who has faith in Jesus Christ, has faith in God the Father. The Father and the Son are one, the Son in the Father, and the Father is in the Son. We behold the glory of the one and only Son of God who was begotten not created. Jesus Christ was with the Father before the creation of the world which means that Jesus Christ was in eternity, and He came to present the people of this world with the eternity.

All the things in Heaven and on Earth were created by Christ, and they were created for Him, by the power of the Holy Spirit, all things were made according to Jesus Christ pleasure for the praises of His holy name and for the holy trinity's glory. Jesus Christ is the consummation of peace forever more because by the power of His Word, Heaven and Earth consists. Jesus Christ is the mediator of a new covenant He is the head of the church, the foundation of the church the corner stone, the first born of all creations. Jesus Christ is the embodiment of the truth, He is the truth in Him all mercies flows, the gift of grace, the strength of all the believers now and Earth and until His returns to Earth. In Jesus Christ all the fullness of God dwell richly. God reconciled us to Himself through Jesus Christ; He adopted us as His children through Jesus Christ, Christ righteousness became our righteousness, God sees all those who believe in Jesus' righteousness believers were cloth with Christ righteousness. The Scripture says: "For in Him we live and move and have our being. As one of your own poets has said, we are His offspring. There for since we are God's offspring we should not think that the divine being s like gold or silver or stone - an image made by main's design and skill. In the past God over looked such ignorance, but now He commands all people everywhere to repent" (Acts 17:28-30). Before Christ came to the world; in time past, before the full knowledge of God became known through Jesus Christ; God over looked sin and many sin nature of human sins and ignorance, or lack of knowledge of God. In these days that the full and perfect revelation of God has come to Earth by Christ Jesus' appearing, all people are commanded to repent and believe in Jesus as Lord and Savior with no exceptions, Jews and the Gentiles, for God will not overlook any one's sins anymore.

All the people of this Earth must turn from their sins to God or be condemned; repentance, in other words, is an essential posture for receiving the gift of salvation. Jesus Christ is the consummation of peace; He put end into God's wrath by blessing us with the Holy Spirit. "He is the image of the invisible God, the first born over all creation. For by Him all things were created; things in Heaven and on Earth, visible and invisible, whether thrones or powers or rulers or authorities; all this were created by Him and for Him. He is before all things, and in Him all things hold together. And He is the head of the body, the church; He is the beginning and the first born from among the dead, so that in everything He might have the supremacy. For God was pleased to have all His fullness dwell in Him, and through Him to reconcile to Himself all things, whether things on Earth or things in Heaven, by making peace through His blood, shed on the Cross" (Colossians 1:15-20) Jesus Christ was the first born - first as the heir of God, we believers a joint heir of God with

Christ first born also men that Christ has the supremacy over all created beings.

Jesus Christ is the heir and blessed ruler of all the souls of people on Earth as the eternal Son of God. Apostle Paul makes it clear the activities of Jesus Christ. All things both spiritual and material things owed their existence to Jesus Christ works as the active agent in creation. In Christ all things were hold together and they were sustained by Him. Jesus Christ was the first to rise from the dead through the power of the resurrection with a spiritual and immortal body. On the resurrection day, Jesus Christ became the head of the church in Heaven and on Earth. The New Testament church, the apostles begin on Christ resurrection Sunday when the disciples received the Holy Spirit, Jesus Christ became the resurrection of all those whom He died and rose and ascended to Heaven. Therefore, the Deity of Jesus Christ in the clear terms, the full and complete Godhead with all that it represents resides in Christ.

The Scripture revealed: "Far above all rule and authority, power and dominion, and every title that can be given, not only in the present age but also in the one to come. And God placed all things under His feet and appointed Him to be head over everything for the church, which is the body, the fullness of Him who fills everything in every way" (Ephesians 1:21-22). The fullness of Jesus Christ dwells in the church as His body. The church potentially must partake of all that Jesus Christ is and possesses for the purpose of continuing His ministry and mission in the world. Christians prayer for the fullness of Christ indicates that the church, is on a journey to spiritual maturity until the awareness of the full potential of attaining to the entire or the whole measure of the fullness of Jesus Christ in their life, ministry and mission of the Gospel of God were attained that God the Holy Spirit will comes in fullness to reproduce the life, ministry services of Jesus Christ through the church which is the auto most goal of the Gospel of Christ.

This is the God the Father's highest desire for every believer in Christ. Apostle Paul's prayer then should be our prayers now that the Holy Spirit might empower believer's work in them in greater measure. The reason for this prayer is that all believing Christians to be increased in the greater measure of the Spirit's impartation is that believers may receive more wisdom, revelation and knowledge concerning God's redemptive purpose for the present and for the future salvation, and that they may experience a more abundant power of the Holy Spirit in their lives which means the Holy Spirit's empowerment in the lives of all believing Christians.

All things are created by Jesus Christ including the angels; therefore they are not to be worship, angels were created beings, created by Christ for Him, and for His pleasure, God takes delight in the angels and in His perfection displayed by them; they are for God's service and for God's use as the angels, as messenger of God, to worship God and minister to Him as well as minister to the people in the world. God sends angels to call on the people of God to serve God and glorify God with their spirit, soul, and body. Moreover, those who are not among the elect angels minister to them through the word of the Gospel. The entire universe is under the care of Jesus Christ until He finished the work of the salvation of the people in the whole world.

The Scripture says: "And having disarmed the power and authorities, He made a public spectacle of them, triumphing over them by the Cross" (Colossian 2:15). Jesus Christ disarmed the powers and authorities, Christ triumphed over Satan by disarming all the demonic powers and authorities by His death on the Cross; all the children of God will shares in this triumph. They not only gain victory over the Earthly troubles and temptations but they also possess in Jesus Christ the authority to wage war against the spiritual forces of evil. Believers also will be able to be let by the Holy Spirit whereby, they will be able to determine the righteousness and wrongness of their actions which is not expressly mentioned in the Word of God; in everything, that they say, do, think, or enjoy, they must ask themselves questions - can it be done or can it result to God's glory. (a) As a believer of Jesus Christ can they do all things such as businesses in the name of the Lord Jesus Christ, asking His blessings on their activities of life. (b) As a believer can they give thanks sincerely to God even on something they ask for in prayers but not yet received. (c) Believers must also be able to ask themselves if they were certain that an approval by Jesus Christ concerning their desires and actions that can easily weaken their sincere convictions of other Christians; and that particular action that they engage in weaken their desire for intimate fellowship with Christ.

God's Word and prayer, they must also examine themselves if their actions will hinder, or weaken their witnessing for Jesus Christ. As children of God; all the believing Christians must separate themselves, consecrated themselves from the world and completely live a life that is pleasing to Christ and follow His commandment obedient to His word; in the Holy Scripture. We read in the scripture where Nehemiah is given glory to God: "You alone are the Lord; you made the heavens, even the highest heavens, and all that is on it, the seas, and all that in the them. You give life to everything, and the multitudes of heavens worship you" (Nehemiah 9:6).

The primary themes of Nehemiah's outstanding prayer are for the glory of God graciously endeavor to provide redemption and salvation to the people of Israel and to the people of the world. God shows His divine love for His people throughout the history of the Earth. Jesus Christ is the consummation of peace forever more let us worship Him, in spirit and in truth and with the spirit of holiness from this Earth to Heaven.

"The seventh angel sounded His trumpet, and there were loud voices in Heaven, which said: 'The kingdom of the world has become the kingdom of our Lord and of His Christ, and He will reign for ever and ever.' And the twenty-four elders, who were seated on their thrones before God, fell on their faces and worshiped God, saying: 'We give thanks to you, Lord God Almighty, the one who is and who was, because you have taken your great power and have begun to reign' " (Revelation 11:15-17). The sounding of the seventh trumpet brings an announcement that the world has become the kingdom of Jesus Christ and He will reign forever. The seventh trumpet could be seen as the return of Jesus Christ.

Summary

Christ is the consummation of peace of this universe; the Scripture revealed: "In the beginning you laid the foundations of the Earth, and the heavens are the work of your hands. They will perish, but you remain, they will all wear out like a garment, like clothing you will change them and they will be change discarded, but you remain the same, and your years will never end" (Psalm 102:25-27). God the Father Almighty laid the foundation apply to Jesus Christ as well as, it speaks about the kingdom of the Lord on Earth, and the work of the Lord in creation, and in His eternity. The Scripture said the present Heaven and Earth will be changed for a brand new Heaven and brand new Earth; but God the Father, Son and the Holy Spirit will never change - God remain the same yesterday, today and forever, He will remain the same. Jesus Christ is the one and only the consummation of peace because of the ministry of forgiveness.

Adam and Eve fall into sin that led all human race into the universal experience of sin, sickness and death. God sent His one and only begotten Son into the world to redeemed human race, all the people in the world through Jesus Christ have their sin wash away through the atonement of Jesus Blood. God therefore, offer the blessings for His people; the blessing of forgiveness of their sins, healing for their diseases, and the gift of redemption as well as eternal life. Forgiveness is the first and most important gift we can receive from God. Through the forgiveness God redeemed all those who believe in Him through Jesus Christ their past, present, and future sins.

Jesus Christ through His divine healing power healed all the diseases of all believers in Him. "He was with God in the beginning. The word became flesh and made His dwelling among us. We have seen His glory, the glory of the one and only, who came from the Father, full of grace and truth" (John 1:1, 14). Apostle John begins His Gospel teaching by calling Christ Jesus the Word of God. By calling Jesus Christ the Word, using this designation for Jesus Christ, presented Him as the personal Word of God as well as indicated that these last days God has spoken to us through His Son. "In the past God spoke to our fore fathers through the prophets at many times and in various ways, but in these last days He has spoken to by His Son, whom He appointed heir of all things and through whom He made the universe" (Hebrews 1:1-2). Now the Lord God Almighty speaking through and revealing Himself through His Son Jesus Christ in a full and complete way. Because our Lord Jesus Christ is supreme over all things, God's Word through Him is full, final and complete and it transcends all the previous words of God.

Absolutely, nothing neither prophets nor Moses has equal authority with the Son of God. Jesus Christ is the only source of eternal salvation and He is the only mediator between God and man. After Jesus Christ provided the forgiveness of our sins by His death and resurrection, He took His place of authority at the right hand of God. Jesus Christ is the perfect revelation of the nature and the person of God. Jesus Christ is the revealer of God the Father; He reveals the innermost heart of the Father. Christ is the manifold wisdom of God; Therefore, Christ redeeming love is incomparable and incomprehensible. Christ Jesus is the true God, the very God He King of kings, the Lord of lords, the God of gods the immortal, the invisible the only wise God. He is the Alpha and the Omega - the Scripture revealed: "I am the Alpha and the Omega says the Lord God, who is and who was, and who is to come, the Almighty" (Revelation 1:8). God the Father, Son and the Holy Spirit ever one God is the beginning and the ending of the universe and all things that is in it, including human history. God is the everlasting and He is from everlasting to everlasting; Christ is the Lord over everything from creation to the consummation of the world history.

Jesus Christ will get the final victory over evil and the demonic wickedness of the people of this world; no one else in all creation. Jesus Christ will set up His kingdom and reign over His people in the new Heaven and the new Earth. "He said to me: it is done. I am the Alpha and the Omega, the beginning and the end. To Him who is thirsty I will give to drink without cost from the spring of the water of life" (Revelation 1:8, 21, 6) God Almighty Himself declares who will inherit the blessings of the new Heaven and the new Earth - those who follow Christ Jesus faithfully throughout their lives will be persevere as Christ's overcomers. They will receive indescribable blessings from this Earth to Heaven and they will forever live with Jesus Christ our Lord and Savior in Heaven; Jesus Christ is the consummation of peace in Heaven and on Earth.

Jesus Christ is the Creator; He was with the Father before the foundation of the world, and Christ was one with the Father and is at the Father's right hand at the present moment; only the Father knows when Christ will be coming back to Earth to establish His Kingdom. God created the heavens and the Earth through Jesus Christ;

everything the Father does all the Trinity is involved with it. Jesus Christ is the Word of God, and He was God, by Him for Him, from Him, and through Him are all things made in the world without end. Amen.

Father and Son and the Holy Spirit worked together in the creation of the universe. One God, the Father from whom all things follows, there is one Son of God Jesus Christ whom all things was created, we move and live and have our being. And the Holy Spirit the giver of life who works with the Father and the Son as the agent in creation. Jesus Christ is the only one who was dead, and raised to life again. He is alive forever there is no other religious leader like Jesus Christ. The other religious leaders were in the grave dead. The meaning of Christianity is based on Jesus Christ crucified, His death, burial and His resurrection, and coming back to judge the people of the world and all the eyes shall see Him.

Jesus Christ is the only Son of God no other religion of the world claiming that their leader is the Son of God. There is no salvation on Earth in any one else only in Jesus Christ the true Son of God. What makes Christianity different from all other world religion is the resurrection of Jesus Christ; His resurrection proofs that power of God in the work of redemption, and in Jesus Christ righteousness.

Jesus Christ is greater than the people in the world and in the Old Testament people Christ is greater than all creations, because of all His miracles, and the power of healing of all diseases because He is the creator.

Jesus Christ is greater than Abraham; Abraham joined the Muslim religion and the Christian religion together through Ishmael and Isaac. Jesus Christ is greater than Jacob because Jesus gives those who believe in Him with the water that springs for eternal life. (John 8:13-14) Jesus is greater than Moses – Christ is the Lawgiver. He gave Moses the Ten Commandments at Mount Sinai. Moses spoke to on the Mount of Sinai and the Mount of transfiguration. Jesus Christ is greater than David; Jesus is the Messiah that was to come, Jesus greater than Melchizek, and King Solomon; He gave King Solomon great wisdom to rule His people, and He blessed Solomon with wealth that made Him the richest King on Earth.

Jesus is greater than Elijah, and Elisha both are servant of Jesus Christ. Jesus is greater than John the Baptist – John the Baptist said: I must decrease and He must increase. Jesus is greater than Sabbath; He said that He created man for Sabbath. Jesus is greater than the church; Jesus is the head of the church, the foundation of the church, the corner stone.   Believers are the church which means the body of Jesus Christ Jesus is greater than the angels because, angels were servants of Jesus Christ, all the things in were servants of Jesus Christ, all the things in Heaven and in Earth will bow down for Jesus as the ruler of the Earth.

Jesus Christ is greater than all other names in Heaven and in Earth in the name of Jesus all the knee shall bow and all the tongue shall confess that Jesus is the Lord to the glory of God" (Philippians 2:9-10). Jesus is He consummation of the consummation of peace believe in Him you will have eternal life. The Scripture says: "Therefore, God exalted Him to the highest place and gave Him the name that is above every names, that at the name of Jesus every knee should bow, in Heaven and on Earth and under the Earth, and every tongue confess that Jesus Christ is the Lord, to the glory of God the Father" (Philippians 2:9-10). God exalted the human nature of Jesus and His divine nature. Christ's exaltation was consist honor and power God wants the whole creation in Heaven and on Earth to be subjected to Jesus and things under the Earth including all the other planets and everything that is in them; including the living and the dead they will hear His voice and get out of the grave.

The glory of God the Father was paid to Him through Jesus Christ His Son. God highly exalted Jesus because He Himself to the point of death, the death on the Cross. The holy name of Jesus Christ must be highly exalted by all the people on Earth. Christ was voluntarily humble Himself during humiliation, pain, suffering and the death on the Cross, Christ remain obedient to His Father's commandment and to the plan of redemptive work for the people of this universe.

"Keep your lives free from the love of money and be content with what you have, because God has said, 'Never will I leave you, never will I forsake you.' So we say with confidence. 'The Lord is my helper; I will not be afraid. What can man do to me' (Hebrews 13:5-6). We have to know that greed and immorality are closely connected; often the love of abundance, luxury constant desire for wealth easily open up a person to sexual sins. The Lord Jesus Christ said: He is our helper, we should not be afraid; He is the all sufficient, all-powerful and all-mighty that will supply all our needs. We must stand on His Rock of salvation forever.

The Confession of Sin

Almighty and most merciful God, Father of our Lord Jesus Christ, Maker of all things, Judge of all men: we acknowledge our sins; we strayed from your ways like lost sheep, our manifold sins and wickedness, which we from time to time most grievously have committed, by thought, words and deeds. We have followed too much the devices and desires of our own hearts; we have offended against Your holy laws; we have left undone those things which we ought to have done, and we have done those things which we ought not to have done, against your divine Majesty; provoking most justly your wrath and indignation against us. We do earnestly repent, and are heartily sorry for these: our misdoings; the remembrance of them is grievous unto us; the burden of them is intolerable. But O' Lord, have mercy upon us, spare those who confess their faults and sins, according to your promises declared unto mankind in Christ Jesus our Lord; and grant our repentance of sins; O' most merciful Father, have mercy upon us, have mercy upon us, most merciful Father , for your Son our Lord Jesus Christ's sake, forgive us all that is past, restore us and grant that we may ever hereafter serve and please you in newness of life, that we may live a godly, righteous life, to the honor and glory of your Holy name, through Jesus Christ our Lord and Savior, Amen.

"The nations were angry; and your wrath has come. The time has come for judging the dead, and for rewarding your servants the prophets and your saints and those who reverence your name, both small and great and for destroying those who destroy the Earth" (Revelation 11:18-19). The dead will be judged and God will destroy those who destroy the Earth, those who are evil, all the evildoers will be judge they will not be in the new earth.

All Denominational Apostle Creed for All People

"I believe in God the Father the Almighty, the maker of heaven and the earth, of all that is seen and unseen. I believe in our Lord Jesus Christ, the true Son of God, the one and only eternally begotten not created of the Father, the God from God, the light from light the true light that shines forever and no darkness can comprehend it. The true God the very God, one with the Father, through the Son all things were created of things in heaven and things on Earth. He came down from heaven for our salvation by the power of the Holy Spirit; He became incarnate from the virgin Mary and was conceived by the Holy Spirit, born of Virgin Mary and was made man. He suffered from Pontius Pilate; He was crucified. He suffered death and was buried. The third day He rose from the dead according to the power of God the Father, who called Him out of the grave. He ascended into Heaven and is seated at the right hand of God the Father. He is coming back in glory to judge the dead and the living and all the eyes shall see Him; His Kingdom on Earth will have no end. I believe in the Holy Spirit, the giver of life, who proceeds from the Father and the Son; the Holy Trinity with the Father and the Son - He is worshiped and glorified. The

Holy Spirit has spoken from the beginning of creation through the prophets and Moses. I believe in the communion of Saints, I acknowledge one baptism for the remission of sins, the resurrection of the body and life everlasting. Amen, Amen, Amen.

The Lord's Prayer

284

"Our Father who at in heaven hallowed be your name, your kingdom come, your will be done on earth as it is written in heaven. Give us each day our daily bread, and forgive us our sins, as we forgive everyone who sins against us. And lead us not into temptation, but deliver us from evil. For thine is your kingdom, your power and your glory now and forever amen."

PRAYER

God the Father Almighty, Father of our Lord Jesus Christ, you are the beginning and the end, the first and the last, the immortal and the invisible the only wise God. There is no one before you our Lord and Savior and no one after you. Jesus Christ you are the true Son of God before the foundation of the world. Jesus Christ you are the one and only the consummation of peace from the beginning of the creation of the universe. Bless all the people in the world with you abundant peace, immeasurable peace.

You are the one and only our heavenly Father: Father, Son, and the Holy Spirit. Manifest your love among the people in all the nations of this world. Bless them with your divine Will that sustain the human life; protect all the people of this world from demonic and Satan's temptation and destructive plans.

Jesus Christ you're the consummation of love bless us with your love; so that we can be able to love you and love our neighbor as we love ourselves. You are the consummation of spiritual power; bless us with the power of the Holy Spirit so that we can be able to live a life that will be pleasing in your sight.

Our Lord and Savior and our redeemer King; you are the consummation of mercy; bless us with your infinite mercy, so that we will be able to worship you as we ought. Lord Jesus Christ you are the consummation of eternal life, bless us with your eternal life so that we will be able to live with you in Heaven forever. God the Father Almighty in the great holy name of Jesus Christ the only consummation of peace I pray accept my prayer. Amen, Amen, Amen

"Then I saw a new Heaven and a new Earth, for the first Heaven and the first Earth had passed away, and there was no longer any sea. I saw the Holy City, the new Jerusalem, coming down out of Heaven from God, prepared as a bride beautifully dressed for her husband" (Revelation 21:1-2). *The final goal and expectation of the redeemed are a new, transformed and redeemed world where Jesus Christ will lives with His people and righteousness dwells in the holy perfection. The new Earth will become the dwelling place of both humans and God.*

Song

Crown Him with many crowns, the Lamb upon His throne;

Hark! How the heavenly anthem drowns all music but its own;

Awake, my soul, and sing of Him who died for three,

And hail Him as thy matchless king through all eternity.

Crown Him the Lord of life, who triumphed o'er the grave,

And rose victorious in the strife for those He came to save;

His glories now we sing who died and rose on high,

Who died eternal life to bring, and lives that death may die.

Crown Him the Lord of Love; behold His hands and side,

rich wounds, yet visible above, in beauty glorified;

no angels in the sky can fully bear that sight,

but downward bends their burning eyes at mysteries so bright.

Crown Him the Lord of years, the potentate of time,

Creator of the rolling sphere, ineffably sublime.

All hail, redeemer, hail! For thou hast died for me;

Thy praise shall never, never fail throughout eternity.

Words: Matthew Bridges, 1851; Music George J Elvey, 1868

Praise God from whom all Blessings Flow, Praise Him all creatures here below, Praise above Ye Heavenly Host, Praise Father, Son and Holy Ghost. Amen

"And I heard a loud voice from the throne saying, Now the dwelling of God is with men, and He will live with them. They will be His people, and God Himself will be with them and be their God. He will wipe every tear from their eyes. There will be no more death or mourning or crying or pain. For the old order of things has passed away" (Revelation 21:3-4). All the redeemed will possess bodies like Christ's resurrection body, ones that are real, visible and tangible, incorruptible and immortal. The new Jerusalem that is already exists in Heaven will come to Earth as the city of God for which Abraham and all of God's faithful waited, and of which God is the architect and the builder.

Biblical Indexes

Genesis 21:33, 1:1-2, 14:18,

Exodus 23:24, 19:6,

Deuteronomy 4:29, 33:27, 14:2, 4:29, 30:20,

Joshua 1:5,

1st Chronicles 29:11, 10:13,

2nd Chronicles 35:36,

Nehemiah 9:6,

Job 1:1-25,

Psalms 33:10, 37:30-31, 86:15, 105:51, 140:12, 10:14, 12:5, 34:17-18, 139:16, 5-6, 23:1-6, 32:1-2, 116:15,25:16, 102:25-27, 103:3-4, 103: 12-13, 16:11, 21:6, 111:10, 119:160, 42:5-6a, 147:11, 24:9-10, 25:16, 102:25-27,

Isaiah 40:9-12, 44:24, 5:16, 9:7, 26:9, 32:17, 42, 6, 21, 45:8, 51:8, 58:8, 11:2, 11:2, 28:29, 5:16, 9:7, 26:9,25:16, 27:10, 34:17, 138:8, 7:14, 1:18, 45:8, 32:17, 42:6, 21, 26:4, 59:16, 40:9-12, 44:24, 22:13b, 33:22, 54:5, 40:31, 11:2, 65:17-19,

Jeremiah 23:16, 29:11

Ezekiel 18:4, 18:40, 20, 31, 48:11, 36:25-27, 11:19,

Zechariah 8:8,

Matthew 10:28, 7:13-14, 18:19-20, 6:11, 10:28, 5:1-48, 6:14-15, 5:44-45, 28:8-10, 19:29, 2:46, 25:21, 23b, 24:45, 24:14, 5:4-5, 12:36

Mark 10:35,

Luke 2:52, 23:43, 2:8-14, 24:1-6, 19:40,1:26-28, 31-33, 1:46-49, 2:6-7, 2:10-11, 2:1, 56, 6-8, 16:22, 25,

John 11:11, 39, 1:57, 5:28, 3:16, 10:10, 3:3, 1:3, 1:15, 1:9, 1:16-17, 16:7, 3:16, 3:36, 4:36, 4:14, 14:16-18, 14:9-11, 1:1, 14,

Acts 6:3, 17:11, 1:3-5, 20:21-22, 7:38-39, 17:12, 17:17, 6, 17:1-2, 5:7-8, 17:17, 6, 17:1-2, 17:2-21, 8:21, 11:25-26, 17:26, 17:28-30, 17:11

Romans 1:17, 3:5,22, 4:3, 9, 13, 14:17, 6:13,16,18-19, 10, 5:17, 3:24, 6:4, 23, 1:16, 20, 8:6-11, 14:10, 8:16-17, 8:8-10, 5:7, 5:3-5, 12:12,5:3-5, 8:28, 11:36,

1st Corinthians 15:22, 51-52, 8:6, 3:11, 14:9, 10:4 1:18, 1:24-25, 1:19, 27, 3:11-15, 1:30-31, 15:12-22,15:40-47, 49, 15:52-54, 1:21-25, 1:9, 4:2-5,

2nd Corinthians 12:7-10, 12:7-10, 1:36, 4:8, 5:21, 5:10, 9:8, 5:10, 5:17, 5:17-21, 3:6,

Galatians 3:28,

Ephesians 6:10-18, 1:10, 2:20, 5, 10, 3:8, 3:9, 1:17, 4:24, 1:10, 2:9-10, 1:21-22, 1:17, 1:17,

Philippians 2:10, 1:11, 3:10,4:7, 1:11, 3:20-21, 2:9-11, 4:7,

Colossians 1:13-18, 1:15, 1:20, 2:3, 2:2, 3:1, 1:19-20, 2:9-10, 1:15-20,

1st Thessalonians 4:14, 13, 5:23,5:16-18, 4:18

2nd Thessalonians

1st Timothy 2:1-2, 2:3-6

2nd Timothy 1:10, 4:8

Hebrews 1:2, 10-12, 3:3-4, 1:8, 5:6, 7:17, 3:3-4, 7:25, 2:18 4:15-16, 13:20-21, 11:10, 12:26-27, 1:1-2,

James 5:16, 1:5, 3:13, 5:20,

1st Peter 3:21,

2nd Peter2:17, 3:13, 3:10,

1st John 2:1, 3:1, 3:2,

Revelation 5:13-14, 13:20, 16:23, 6:23, 20:11-15, 22:17, 5:13-14, 7:14-17, 4:1, 1:8, 1:8, 21, 6,

"He who as seated on the throne said, 'I am making everything new!' Then He said, 'Write this down, for these words are trust worthy and true.' He said to me; 'It is done, I am Alpha and the Omega, the Beginning and the End. To Him who is thirsty I will give to drink without cost from the spring of the water of life. He who overcomes will inherit all this, and I will be His God and He will be my son" (Revelation 21:5-7). The evil things of the first Heaven and Earth have completely passed away. Believers, will evidently not remember that which would cause them sorrow anymore. God Himself declares who will inherit the blessings of the new Heaven and the new Earth – those who faithfully persevere as Christ's overcomers.

Bibliography

<u>The Student Bible New Revised Standard Version</u> by Philip Yancey and Tim Stafford Zondervan Corporation 1994, 1996 Grand Rapids, Michigan 49530 USA.

<u>Evangelical Dictionary of Biblical Theology</u> Walter A. Elwell Published by Baker Books a Division of Baker Book House Company Grand Rapids, Michigan 49516-6287.

<u>Matthew Henry's Commentary In One Volume</u>, Zondervan Publishing House A Division of Harper Collins Publishers Rev. Leslie F. Church, Ph.D. .r. Hist.S. Marshall, Morgan and Scott Ltd 1960 Grand Rapids, Michigan 49530.

<u>Believer's Bible Commentary a Complete Bible Commentary in One Volume</u> William MacDonald, Art Farstad 1979 Thomas Nelson Publishers Nashville Tennessee.

<u>Systematic Theology Volume Four Church Last Things</u>, Dr. Norman Geisler, 2005 Bethany House Minneapolis, Minnesota.

<u>Exploring the New Testament</u>, Ralph Earle, Th.D. Harvey J. S. Blaney, Th.M. Carl Hanson, Th.D. Beacon Hill Press 1955 Kansas City, Missouri USA.

McDowell, Edward A. The Meaning and message of the Book of Revelation, Nashville: Broadman, Press, 1951.

Gore, Charles. The Epistle of St. John. New York Charles Scribner's sons, 1920.

Ross, Alexander. The Epistle of James and John in the new International commentary on the New Testament. Grand Rapids; Wm. B. Eardmans Publishing Co., 1954.

Newell, William R. The Book of Revelation. Chicago; Grace Publications, 1935.

The Interpretation of Scripture by James D. Smart the Westminster Press Philadelphia 1946.

Warfield, B. B., Revelation and Inspiration, Oxford University Press, 1927.

The New Testament an Expanded Translation Volume I the Gospel 1956 Kenneth S. Wuest William B. Eerdmans Publishing company Grand Rapids, Michigan.

Living Doctrines of the New Testament H. D. Donald DD Ph.D. Zondervan Publishing House Grand Rapids 1972 USA.

Murray, J. Redemption Accomplished and Applied 1955, William Eerdmans Publishing Company Grand Rapids, USA.

Telfer, W., The Forgiveness of Sins SCM Press London, 1959.

"He who testifies to these things says Yes, I am coming soon. Amen, Come, Lord Jesus" (Revelation22:20). Jesus Christ promised that He is coming soon, to which John responds, "Come Lord Jesus." This longing is shared by all the true Christians all over the world. It is a prayer of confession that, until He comes, our redemption remains incomplete, evil and sin are not yet over-thrown and this world is not yet renewed. Jesus Christ is the consummation of peace in a new Heaven and a new Earth where only righteous dwell.

Books previously Published by the author:
Grace Dola Balogun
by
Grace Religious Books Publishing & Distributors, Inc.

New York

PRAYER THE SOURCE OF STRENGTH FOR LIFE -

English Edition

Prayer the Source of Strength for Life is a powerful book that will energize your spirit to pray more and more until the prayer is part of your life and until the gate of Heaven is opened and your prayer is answered. Your prayer life will change your life.

LA ORACION FUENTE DE FORTALEZA PARA LA VIDA – Spanish Edition.

Dios no's dio el poder de la oracion, quiere que lo usemos; debemos illamar, comunicarnos con el en todo lo que estemo spasando. El espera saber denosotros.

Spirit Power Volumes I and II

Spirit Power Volumes I and II both discuss the power of the Holy Spirit in the lives of believers.

The Power of the Spirit of God begins from the creation of the world up until today. That power will also continue until Christ returns to reign. Hallelujah

THE CROSS AND THE CRUCIFIXION

Our Lord Jesus Christ died on the Cross to bring forth love and compassion. Sin's impact on human life brings all other evil into our world, from one society to another society, from one culture to another.

But in Christ, we are clothed with His holiness. We have the gift of eternal life. The gate of Heaven is open and we are eligible for our inheritance in Heaven.

Hallelujah! Hosanna in the Highest. Jesus Christ paid it all, unto Him all we owe. The Cross of Christ is the Cross of joy, peace, and righteousness to all who believe in Him.

THREE SIMPLE SOLUTIONS FOR WORLD PEACE

Three Simple Solutions for World Peace is a book that clears all the confusion that many people of the world have been going through for many years. It is a book that gives light and advice to some of the problems that plague the world, and that offers solutions for these problems. It is a book that is full of knowledge, understanding and solutions that will bring some peace to the world.

Justification by Faith Alone in Christ Alone

Justification by Faith Alone in Christ Alone will clear all the confusion of believers' faith in Jesus Christ. Believers will also rejoice in the long sufferings – they will rejoice in their sufferings, afflictions, persecutions, rejections and all various trials that may press in on them because these long-sufferings will help all the believers to be redeemed in Christ.

CHRISTIAN CELL PHONE SERIES:

Christian Cell Phone Godly Wisdom helps readers understand the role of God's wisdom and the importance of obtaining godly wisdom in one's life to produce prosperous results in all areas of life. These areas are critical and include family, relationships and finances. The acquiring of God's wisdom is to be sought after in life and will impact others as well.

Christian Cell Phone God's Favor is designed to give readers knowledge of God's favor from the Old Testament to the New Testament. With an analysis of the favor that was on Jesus, the Son of God, the reader will find that God's favor can completely change one's life and lead others to Christ as well.

Christian Cell Phone God's Anointing takes a look at the anointing on the life of Jesus that includes present day believers in Christ Jesus. This anointing can be applied to all areas of life and can be seen in miraculous ways. The anointing is what makes our life incredible and supernatural, drawing all those who see, to Christ.

JESUS CHRIST THE JOY OF CHRISTMAS

Jesus Christ the Joy of Christmas gives praise and tribute to the child that was born in Bethlehem. Tracing the prophecies of Old about this King that was born, the author gives an account of the sinless Lamb of God who came to take away the peoples' sin from a biblical perspective, who is the real Joy of Christmas.

PRAYER FOR THE BULLY VICTIMS AND THE BULLY TOO!

Prayer for the Bully Victims and the Bully Too addresses the issue of the bully from the classroom to the home. By the use of scriptural application, the author takes a look at what can be done to help the bully kid and their victims. The author has written several key prayers that readers can use to help either the bully victim or parents who are dealing with a child that has become a bully.

I AM THE RESURRECTION AND THE LIFE

I Am The Resurrection and The Life: Powerful, inspirational and written from a firm biblical perspective, multi-published author Grace Dola Balogun, gives life to others through the power of Jesus Christ who is the Resurrection and the life. This book will open eyes to the amazing and abundant blessings of accepting Jesus Christ as your Lord and Savior, giving keen insight into the Scriptures on the power available to all through the Holy Spirit with an emphasis on aspects of eternal life for the believer.

I AM THE ETERNAL LIFE

I Am The Eternal Life: Encouraging, uplifting and filled with a sound biblical perspective, this book encourages believers and non-believers alike to look to the One that is Jesus Christ, the Son of God, who is the Bread of life and the one who gives eternal life to all who believe in Him. This book gives readers a heavenly perspective on their life, revealing believer's God-given destiny and purpose to all who call on Jesus Christ as their Lord and Savior. The truth of the Gospel and the Good News is eloquently displayed in this delightful and insightful read.

HE WHO BELIEVES IN ME SHALL NEVER DIE

He Who Believes In Me Shall Never is a fascinating teaching, revealing Jesus as the way, the truth and the life - the Everlasting life. All who believe in Him shall never die. Beginning from the Old Testament, the author takes a look at the fall of humanity through the sin of disobedience through Adam and Eve. Comparing this fall to the sin of disobedience today, the author reveals scriptural truths in the lives of Enoch, Elijah and Moses. The author gives insight into the baptism of the Holy Spirit and gives examples of the Spirit's power and the purpose for which the power is given to believers. The author has given key scriptural insights that all who believe in Jesus Christ will have everlasting life in Him that continues to Heaven.

FORGIVE OUR DEBTS AS WE FORGIVE OUR DEBTORS

Forgive Our Debts As We Forgive Our Debtors speaks of divine forgiveness from the Lord and the Lord's commandment to forgive others, including ourselves. With the Lord's Prayer as a foundation, author Grace D. Balogun, explores from the Old Testament to the New Testament meanings of forgiveness and the consequences of sin. The author gives keen biblical insight into the subject of forgiveness, bringing life-changing healing that is only acquired through the power of forgiveness.

She must be Silent: The Great Commission Bestowed on Both Men and Women is a controversial book that takes a look at the role of women throughout biblical history and gives key scriptural insight into the role of women from the Old Testament to the New Testament. An encouraging, enlightening read, this book is recommended for women and men that want to understand the role of women from a biblical perspective. This book does an excellent job in giving insight into key roles that women play in God's redemptive plan and sheds light on the empowerment of the Holy Spirit that is given to both men and women by God, who is no respecter of persons.

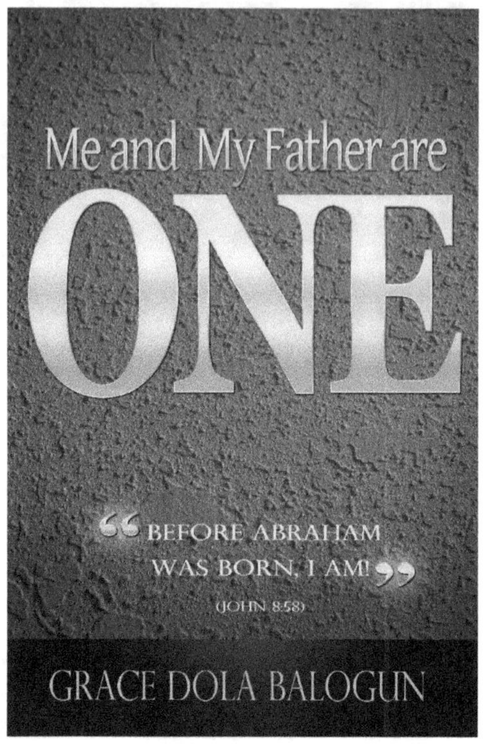

Me and My Father Are One: Before Abraham was Born, I Am (John 8:58) explains that God the Father and Jesus Christ are one from the beginning. In this book, the reader will learn that the plan of redemption is from the Father and is carried out through His Son, Jesus Christ, who is the Word of God. In the beginning, before Abraham, before Adam and Eve, Christ says, "I Am." Written from a biblical perspective, the author displays that Jesus Christ was in the beginning and as Scripture says, "He is before all things, and in Him all things hold together" (Colossians 1:17).

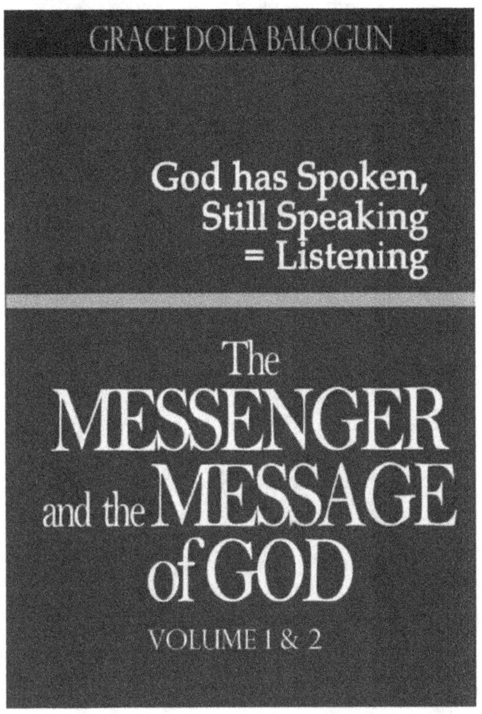

The Messenger and the Message of God (Volumes I & 2) systematically offers the message of God spoken through the prophets of Old and Christ's disciples in the gospels, to include the mission of Paul the Apostle. For use as an individual study or within a group setting, these volumes are recommended to gain understanding of certain books of the prophets and the New Testament gospels. *Volume I* is focused on selected prophets of the Old Testament and *Volume II* relates the disciples and their callings in the gospels of the New Testament. God has spoken, is still speaking today and we are to listen to Him, heeding the message.

Be Holy for I Am Holy - God has created and redeemed all of the Christian believers; we belong to Him, and we have passed through troubles and afflictions. We will not be destroyed, for He is with us. We are precious and honored in His sight; believers are the objects of His great love. God loved us before He put us in the womb and brought us into this world. God will never forsake His people. He would continue His love for they would still be a special people reserved for mercy. The expressions of God's goodwill to His people here speak abundance of comfort to all of the spiritual children of upright Jacob who are praying for Israel. Through God's care and concern for His people, God created the people of Israel especially for Himself. He made them into a people; God incorporated them by His covenant—purchased and redeemed them. It is the same way with those who are redeemed by the blood of His Son, Jesus Christ.

Christ's Life in the Life of Christians - This book will help you to understand your position in Jesus Christ as a Christian. Reading this book will also give clear understanding of who Christ is in the life of believing Christians. It will give you more divine ability as well as the power of the indwelling of the Holy Spirit that Christ gave to all who believe and gave their life to Him. Jesus Christ is the one who initiates and the one who establishes the New Covenant and His heavenly ministry is far beyond and far more superior to the ministry of Old Testament priests. The New Covenant is an agreement, promise, the last will and testament and a statement of intention to be bestow divine grace and blessing on all those who believe in God; those who in sincere repentance and through faith accept Jesus Christ as the true Son of God.

Remember the Poor & Needy Among Us will help all the believing Christians to learn how important it is to give to the poor, the needy and the sick. Christians must give part of what God provides for them to increase the work of the Lord on this Earth, to reach the people of the entire world for Jesus Christ in their own language. Christians must set apart for God every day, part of their income, and other natural resources to honor God and to enhance the work of the Kingdom of God on this Earth. They must also give their resources to charity, to the poor, so that the poor may have something to eat and be satisfied. When you make a feast, or doing any celebration, invite the poor and the needy. People who are unable to pay you back because they were unable to work for a living. By feeding them, clothing them, helping them, these types of charity are the true charity.

All Churches Be One - Jesus came to this world to save sinners and the lost, to join people in the world together with His divine love. Our Lord and Savior gives the purpose of His Spirit anointed ministry to the people in the synagogue. God the Father sent Him to preach the Gospel to the poor, the sinners, the afflicted, the humble, the destitute and to those who are crushed in spirit; the brokenhearted and those who tremble at His Word. Christ said that He was sent to heal those who are bruised and oppressed; the healing of Jesus Christ consists of physical and spiritual healing. All churches must adopt Christ's message, words, preaching and teaching. They must preach the Gospel of God exactly as Christ taught and preached it; without adding to it, or taking away from it. This book will open the hearts and minds of all the believing Christians in a way that they will worship the Lord with the Spirit of truth and holiness so that they will come to the knowledge and understanding that God the Father, God the Son and God the Holy Spirit is One God - the Holy Trinity ever one God.

The Church: The Body of Christ shows how those who gave their life to Jesus Christ are one in Him as He is one with the Father. They renounced, put aside sin and the flesh, they walk in the full protection of Jesus Christ Himself. The book also deals with the three observable manifestations at Pentecost that correspond exactly to the three forces promised of the risen Lord to His disciples regarding the power to witness to all the people in the world. This book also expounds the events of the Day of Pentecost, which shows Christ's Disciples that their Master, Jesus Christ, was fulfilling His word of promise from His ascended position at the right hand of God in Heaven.

GOD'S ELECTION: Who Shall Lay Anything to the Charge of God's Elect (Romans 8:33)

God's Election will help the reader to gain a clear and accurate understanding of God's desires and purpose for His beloved creation – mankind. Before the foundation of the world, God had a purpose for all mankind. This book will help the reader to gain knowledge and understanding of God's plan for one's life. No matter what God has designed for you, and the task He places before you in your life, believe that God's promise of His divine abiding presence and help will never fail you; therefore, remain steadfast in your faith. Eye- opening and inspiring boost your faith, make your spirit strong in His righteousness and the gift of salvation through Jesus Christ. Gain the incomparable love of Jesus Christ, our Lord and Savior, whom God the Father elected before the foundation of the world to take away the sins of the whole world through His death on the cross and His resurrection.

God's Predestination "For Those He Foreknew, He Also Predestined" (Romans 8:29) - a delightful read that takes one through the God of mercy from the Old Testament to the New Testament wherein God watched over the Israelites in the desert, leading up to God's grace in that He bestowed His mercy to all, that they might become children of God. Encouraging and insightful, many chapters present the inheritance of the believer as they become more Christ-like in the power of the Holy Spirit

ABOUT THE AUTHOR

Grace Dola Balogun graduated from Fordham University Graduate School of Religion and Religious Education in the year 2010 with an M.A. in Religion and Religious Education. She has been a prayer mentor and advisor for many Christians of all denominations for many years.

Visit her online at: www.Gracereligiousbookspublishers.com

Facebook - https://www.facebook.com/grace.d.balogun

Twitter - https://twitter.com/prayersource

To order additional copies of this book, please E-mail: info@gracereligiousbookspublishers.com.

This book may also be ordered from 30,000 wholesalers, retailers, and booksellers in the U. S., and in Canada and over100 countries globally.

To contact Grace Dola Balogun for an interview or a speaking engagement, please E-mail:

info@gracereligiousbookspublishers.com

The Spirit and the bride say,

"Come!" And let the one who hears say, "Come!" Let the one

who is thirsty come;

and let the one who wishes take the free

gift of the water of life (Revelation 22:17).

MARANATHA EVEN SO COME LORD JESUS (1ST
CORINTHIANS 16:22, REVELATION 22:20)

326

<u>ORDER FORM</u>

327

TO ORDER YOUR COPY OF ANY BOOK:

NAME:_______________________________

ADDRESS:____________________________

____

TELEPHONE:__________________________

FAX#:_______________________________

MAIL:_______________________________

QUANTITY:___________________________

<u>MAIL TO:</u>

Grace Religious Books Publishing & Distributors, Inc.
New York
213 Bennett Avenue
New York, NY 10040